DESCENDANTS OF THE GLASS PALACE

AN ADVENTUROUS FANTASY

NEETA RAVARIYA

Made with ♥ on the Notion Press Platform
www.notionpress.com

Contents

Introduction

The Glass Palace which was a symbol of friendship between two kings. However, it always remained under the evil eyes of their ministers. To conspire against the kings, to snatch their kingdoms and make the Glass Palace a symbol of their victory, the ministers tried to poison the kings against each other and they tried to sever their alliance, but they failed in their conspiracy and were imprisoned.

However, both the ministers managed to escape and once again sought to harm the kings and eventually succeeded in overthrowing both dynasties. The children of the kings, unable to defend their fathers' thrones, fled the palace. Choosing to abandon their royal heritage, they opted for a life of simplicity. However, an unforeseen event occurred: King Harishan's restless spirit began to visit his grandchildren in their dreams, revealing their true lineage and the legacy of the Glass Palace, with the hope that they would restore the kingdom and safeguard their people from the wicked usurpers.

The king's strategy bore fruit, and upon learning their lineage, the grandchildren vowed to reclaim their ancestral lands and the Glass Palace, by any means necessary. Years later, after getting trained by their Grandsire, the heirs confronted the malevolent new kings, the offspring of the treacherous ministers, leading to an epic conflict.

Madhuraj

Grandsire Vasud
King Harishan
Queen Vedarsha
Aparvi
Parthan
(Son)
Srishtika
(Daughter)
Anishiv
Aravir
(Son)
Ashmi
(Daughter)
Sriha
(Daughter)
Sarath
(Son)

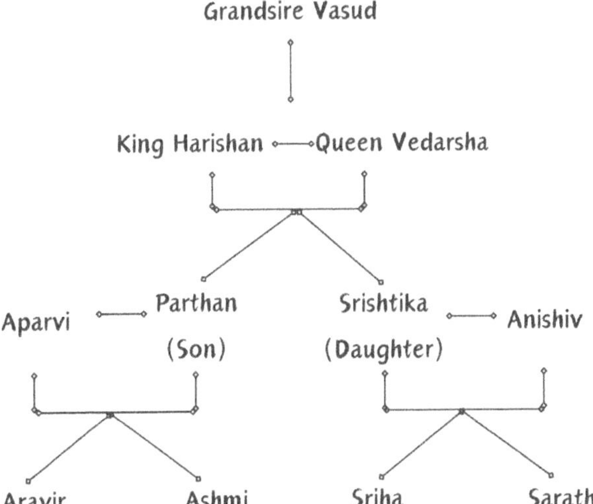

Kushalraj

Grandsire Kavir
King Ashan
Queen Kauriya
Parthan
Aparvi
(Daughter)
Anishiv
(Son)
Srishtika
Aravir
(Son)
Ashmi
(Daughter)
Sriha
(Daughter)
Sarath
(Son)

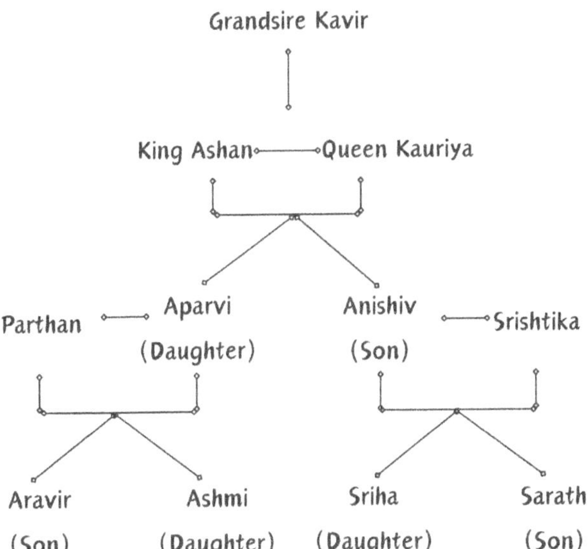

ONE

THE NIGHTMARE

When the mist atmosphere turned into a clear vision. Srishtika saw her father, King Harishan, standing in front of her. Looking at his expression, it seemed like he was agitated. His eyes conveyed a wealth of emotion. Srishtika could clearly see the disappointment etched in her father's eyes, but the reason behind it was a mystery to her.

She asked her father in a concerned voice, "What's wrong, Dad? Why are you looking so upset?"

"I did not expect this from you, Srishtika!" King Harishan responded with a stern tone.

Confusion clouded Srishtika's face; she had no idea what the king was talking about.

Looking at her bewildered look, he elaborated, "You four had promised us that you all would save our heritage, yet I see no effort from you all. Why? Have you all forgotten your promise, your duties towards the throne, or have you no interest in our legacy anymore?"

"No! I haven't forgotten anything. We remember our promises. But as you know, the kingdom is under the enemy's rule. And when a person becomes a king, he gets power along with the throne. The power to rule the kingdom as he wishes!" She answered.

"But no power is greater than a good intention, princess! The king is powerful because of his throne. Therefore, our forefathers used to appoint the king based on his merits and prowess, and this principle is still upheld. If your intentions are good, you can also challenge the king's rules if they are unjust. The first duty of the king is to serve his people, to think about their well-being and happiness before his own desires and needs. Furthermore, if a king neglects his duties, he doesn't deserve the throne. You're well aware that Tushyan and Shangir have betrayed us, and the throne of our kingdom has been snatched from us. They are using the throne's power for their own selfish desires. As the royal offspring, it's your responsibility to protect our heritage, but you, Parthan, Aparvi, and Anishiv have forgotten it completely." King Harishan said.

"We tried our best, but we were no match for those powerful rulers. Right now, they hold more power. We also have children, and putting their lives at risk is not an option; they could harm our families."

The king answered angrily, "Do you really think that your children will be proud to learn about your past, that you didn't even try to save your kingdom and instead sat at home like a fool? Are the people of the kingdom not your responsibility? Is it not your duty to fulfill your forefathers' desires?"

"I'm not a fool!" She felt as though his words were ripping her heart apart. Her eyes became numb.

"Will you let our legacy fall into the wrong hands so easily?" He paused for a moment while looking at her.

He sought answers in her eyes that could give peace to his soul. However, he found nothing but perplexity. Srishtika couldn't answer his questions. She was standing silently.

"My soul will find peace only when my kingdom is in safer hands. I can't wait any longer." King Harishan's voice trembled with sorrow. He felt a lump in his throat and was unable to speak.

King Harishan thought she would understand and would do something for her lineage, but Srishtika had nothing to say; she remained silent. King Harishan's heart ached, and he sternly stated,

"Now, your descendants will witness the tale of our kingdom and their parents' past with their own eyes. Also, remember one more thing, this will surely happen with not only your kids but also your brother's children."

"No! Please don't do this! They are just teenagers. They won't be able to handle it. I beg of you, do not disclose anything to them."

"Royal offspring must be strong. They must never forget their duties to the kingdom. My grandchildren are also part of the royal lineage. They should be aware of our kingdom's history. However, you are insisting so much; I will make it a little easier for you. So that you can get some time to consider." He took a deep breath and resumed talking.

"Your children will see your past as their previous life. They won't realize that whom they are considering as their previous life is actually their parents' past life. Those four children will make four of you realize your duties and your responsibilities as royal offspring. I was here to give you a reminder about your responsibilities. Goodbye!" He said and disappeared in the blink of an eye.

Srishtika woke up with a jerk from her deep sleep and realised it was just a dream. She pondered over it, wondering if the king had tried to convey something to her in the dream or if it was just an illusion.

"I have to discuss this matter with Parthan, Aparvi and Anishiv." She thought to herself.

A few moments later, Parthan, Aparvi, and Anishiv were gathered at Srishtika's home, summoned by her urgent call. Srishtika was standing in front of them, her expression was grave.

"What happened, Srishtika? Why did you call us here in such a hurry, and why do you look petrified?" Parthan asked.

Taking a deep breath, Srishtika responded with a serious tone, "Soon, our children will learn everything about the Glass Palace and our past."

Immediately, the atmosphere shifted, and everyone's expressions turned into worry.

"What? How? When?" Aparvi asked, her voice filled with worry.

"My father, King Harishan, told me in a dream last night. He revealed that we have neglected our duties, so he will show our children our entire past. I requested him not to say anything to our children, because they will be shocked as they are just teenagers. So, he said that our children will not know that what they are seeing is their parents' past. They will comprehend our past as the story of their previous birth. They will not know about it until we ourselves tell them the truth." Said Srishtika.

"What's the point of doing this?" Anishiv questioned.

"So that we can get some time to think about our responsibilities and realise our duties towards them." Srishtika answered.

"How will King Harishan do all this?" Aparvi asked.

"I don't know! He didn't mention anything about it."

"It might be an illusion. After all, it was just a dream. We are not sure whether this dream is true or not." Said Aparvi.

"No, it can't just be a dream. King Harishan used to love the people of his kingdom and always cared for them. He could sense people's suffering just by looking into their eyes and become restless until he solved their problems.

As we all know that Kushalraj and Madhuraj kingdoms are currently under the control of the ministers' children. They could have seized the Glass Palace too, but they're unable to do so. However, they still have their evil eye on the Glass Palace. Those cunning people are just looking for the right opportunity to take over the Glass Palace." She said irefully.

She took a deep breath to control her anger and further said, "So, just imagine how distressed my father's soul must be after seeing his people in pain."

"Srishtika, I know King Harishan's soul must be suffering, but what can we do? Luck is not on our side right now! Otherwise, I have neither forgotten my responsibilities, nor will I ever forget them in life. I can never see the end of my dynasty. I'm just waiting for the right time and opportunity. However, King Harishan has told you that our children will witness our entire past, so he must have given it some significant thought. Let's just wait and see what destiny has in store for us." Parthan tried to soothe her.

Parthan decided to accept the situation as it was. He had understood that King Harishan wanted to carry forward his legacy, therefore Parthan chose to honour his decisions and his emotions.

"I'm only concerned about our kids. You are aware of how harsh, cruel and unyielding these current rulers are! We had attempted to oppose them, but we failed miserably, suffered injuries, and had to flee the palace." Srishtika expressed.

"I understand! But that one incident cannot break our courage. That's why King Harishan wants our children to know how royalty should present themselves and prioritize their responsibilities over their personal wishes."

Parthan was right, so, unanimously they all decided to wait and watch how their children would find out about their past. They also decided to withhold any information about Srishtika's dream until they get to know everything.

After a few days, Sriha and Aravir approached their mother Srishtika and asked,

"We have a three-day holiday. Can we please visit the beach?"

"No! We can't go to the beach. We can go somewhere else."

Aravir persisted, "But I adore the sea and am eager to explore such places. I want to go there only. Please mom!"

"I said no! If you wish to go somewhere else, that's fine, but we won't go to a place which has water, understand?" She responded sternly and left.

"I don't get it! What's the issue? Why does she never allow me to go to water related places? Whenever I mention the beach, she becomes agitated." Aravir voiced his confusion to Sriha.

Srishtika overheard their conversation while standing outside the room.

"I understand you love the ocean, but you're not allowed to visit places related to water. The same applies to Sriha, I can't allow her to go where wind flows faster. There are certain things you children don't need to know about for your own safety. You both must trust your mother."

As the days went by, Srishtika's restlessness grew, but she remained silent as all four of them chose to remain silent. Days turned into weeks, yet there was no indication of their children finding out the truth. Srishtika began to believe it was all just a figment of their imagination, and their children would remain oblivious to the truth. As time passed, Srishtika, Anishiv, Parthan, and Aparvi completely forgot about the dream.

A month later, Sriha found herself standing before a magnificent mountain, lush with greenery and flowers. There was a rugged path leading up the mountain. She was deeply captivated by its beauty. Suddenly, she noticed two shadows approaching her, which made her nervous. She turned around to see who they were. There she saw a man and a woman standing there.

"You must come to the rescue of your palace." The man said in his deep voice. He was not clearly visible.

"I can no longer bear this deception and the pain it causes." A woman whined.

Sriha, who was standing and eavesdropping on their conversation, was puzzled by the unfolding events. Both the man and woman were pleading with her to help them and their kingdom. She couldn't make out their faces clearly. The sounds of their voices were reverberating around her, causing her distress. She couldn't cope with the situation and covered her ears with her hands. In the midst of all that chaos she fainted.

After a while, she opened her eyes in a jolt and was breathing heavily. That's when she realized she was in her bed and dreaming. It was a nightmare!

Sriha, an 18 years old young woman, was asleep when she experienced this nightmare. It frightened her. Yet, she didn't take it seriously. She shook it off and got ready for college. This had never happened with her before. This was the first time she had such a bizarre dream. Sriha was known for her charm and politeness. She was loved by everyone for her kind nature. She was the daughter of Srishtika and Anishiv.

She went on with her daily routine. After a busy day, she had dinner and went to bed. But as she drifted off to sleep, those same glimpses appeared in her dream, those fleeting visions that were unclear. All she could see was a vague figure. The same man and woman were asking her to save their kingdom. Their voices echoed around her, causing her to wake up abruptly. Days went by like this. That dream had become a regular part of her life, disrupting her sleep. She seemed to have lost her spark. Her mother, Srishtika, noticed these changes in her daughter's behaviour.

One day, Sriha was sitting at her study table, twirling a pen between her fingers. Her gaze was fixed on the statue of the lord at the corner of the table instead of her textbook. When her mother walked by her room, she noticed her. She thought about asking her what was bothering her.

"Are you okay, Sriha?"

As soon as she heard her mother's voice, she looked up and responded, "Hm??"

"What's wrong? For the past few days, I've noticed a change in your behaviour. Where are you lost? Did something happen to you? Is your health all right? Tell me what's troubling you, Sriha?" Her mother asked out of concern.

Sriha didn't answer. She was determined not to mention anything about her dream to her mother until she had all her doubts cleared. Otherwise, her mother would worry.

"Hey! Where are you lost?" Her mother snapped her finger at her face to bring her out of thoughts.

Sriha emerged from her own world, exclaiming, "Nothing, Mom, my exams are coming, that's why I'm a bit stressed, that's it! You don't need to worry, I'm okay!"

Her mother thought, maybe she was overthinking. That's why she nodded and left the room, choosing not to delve deeper into the matter.

The next morning, as usual, Sriha went to college and sat on her bench in the class. She was lost in her thoughts, trying to make sense of her mysterious dreams.

A girl with Hazel brown eyes and curly hair walked into the classroom with her cheerful and confident demeanor. She was Sriha's age. The girl, named Ashmi, was a close friend of Sriha and the daughter of Parthan and Aparvi. As soon as she spotted Sriha, she rushed over and greeted her with a bright smile.

"Good morning, Sriha!"

Ashmi noticed Sriha didn't respond, so she greeted her again, this time a bit louder.

"Good morning, Sriha!"

Ashmi was surprised by Sriha's silence, so she moved closer and placed her hand on Sriha's shoulder, she asked,

"Hey! What's going on? Where are you lost?"

Sriha suddenly snapped back to reality and asked, "Ashmi! When did you get here?"

"What! I greeted you twice, but you didn't respond. What's happening? Are you okay?" Ashmi inquired.

"Maybe!" Sriha replied with a lackluster tone.

"Maybe?" Ashmi mumbled, "Can you please tell me what's bothering you?" She asked.

"Even, I'm not sure what's wrong with me. I've been having the same dream for the past few days. The one with the blurred vision, the foggy weather, and the person crying and pleading for help. They've been betrayed. Maybe that's why they are requesting me to save them. I don't understand what's happening to me!" Sriha was looking puzzled.

Ashmi listened to her while shifting her position on the bench beside Sriha, but as soon as Sriha's words reached her ears, she felt a sense of numbness. She slowly looked at Sriha and asked,

"You too?"

Sriha turned her head towards Ashmi, her expression one of surprise. She asked, "What do you mean by you too?"

"I mean, I'm also experiencing the same terrifying dreams for the past few nights, along with the same hazy vision, misty weather, and those tear-stained faces!" Ashmi replied.

Both the girls gasped; their eyes were wide open in shock. They exchanged glances, clearly taken aback by the situation. This was something that left them both speechless.

"Then why didn't you mention this to me before?" Sriha asked.

"I figured it was just a dream, so I just brushed it off!" Ashmi responded.

The girl seated on the bench behind Sriha and Ashmi was eavesdropping on their conversation. Her name was Risha. Risha was notorious for her love of meddling in others' affairs, spreading gossip like wildfire. Her classmates often referred to her as the "Running Gossip Queen."

"It's okay, guys; dreams are just visualizations of our thoughts. What we think during the day, we see at night. It's as simple as that!" Risha interjected.

"Oh! Is that so? Thank you for enlightening us, Risha ma'am! We had no idea!" Ashmi said, her tone laced with sarcasm.

"We were both trying to ignore the dream, thinking it was just a dream, but we've been having the same one every night. It's not as simple as you make it sound!" Sriha added.

Risha frowned, then moved away. Ashmi and Sriha also turned around. After that, Ashmi leaned closer to Sriha and whispered.

"Let her go, Sriha. Just remember, don't talk about our dream when she's around. Otherwise, she will add her own spice and spread it in class. You know what kind of trouble she can stir up. Be careful!"

"Yes, you're right! I'll keep that in mind next time."

Just then, a woman walked into the classroom, and she was their instructor. Her name was Miss Sarati. All the students stood up to welcome her. Miss Sarati began her lesson. Sriha and Ashmi leaned their books close to their faces, so that the teacher couldn't see them talking. They were whispering to each other.

"Could this be happening to Aravir and Sarath as well?" Ashmi whispered.

"I don't think so! How could four of us have a similar nightmare? I don't think it is possible."

At that time, both the girls didn't realize when Miss Sarati came and stood behind them. Miss Sarati was paying her full attention to listen to their conversation. However, both the girls were speaking softly. Therefore, she could barely hear the last two words. She strained to listen more, but the girl sitting next to Ashmi, hit her foot to Ashmi intentionally. Ashmi immediately turned to look at her. The girl then made a gesture with her eyes, indicating Miss Sarati was behind them. Sriha also noticed her gesture. Both girls became frightened and quickly stood up, glancing over at Miss Sarati.

"What were you two discussing?" Miss Sarati asked in a suspicious tone.

"N…Nothing ma'am!" Sriha stuttered while answering to her.

Miss Sarati was on the verge of asking them more questions, but the bell rang. It was their break time, so everyone, including Ashmi and Sriha, left the classroom. Both girls almost sprinted out of the room. Miss Sarati took two steps forward, deep in thought.

"Similar nightmare!" Those were the only words she had heard. "I have to keep an eye on them." She murmured.

On the other side, Ashmi and Sriha came out of the classroom and sighed with relief.

"Thank God! The bell saved us." Ashmi exclaimed, panting heavily.

"But don't you find Miss Sarati's behavior odd? I mean, how curious she was about what we were talking about. That's quite strange!" Sriha was skeptical about Miss Sarati's behaviour.

"It might be, I don't think she would have any interest in our matter. Right now, I'm eager to speak with Aravir and Sarath." Ashmi ignored Miss Sarati's odd behavior and left with Sriha.

Here, Miss Sarati overheard everything. She was eavesdropping on their conversation from afar, and her suspicion was confirmed.

"There's definitely something fishy going on! Those girls definitely know something about that mystery. I have to find out the truth. If what I'm thinking is correct, then It's the right time to take them to that place.' Miss Sarati mused.

She didn't realize that both the girls had left when she was engrossed in her thoughts. She wanted to know more, that's why, she slowly leaned a bit to catch a glimpse of them but found no one there.

"Oh no! Again, I missed the chance." She banged her fist on the pillar in frustration.

Aravir was the older brother of Ashmi and the son of Parthan and Aparvi. Sarath was the older brother of Sriha and the son of Srishtika and Anishiv. Both Aravir and Sarath were close friends. Thus, the four children were not only first cousins but also neighbours. From their childhood, they had developed a deep connection. Aravir and Sarath were two years older than Ashmi and Sriha. They were unaware of their familial ties; all they knew was they were neighbours.

Their parents wanted to hide their real identity from their children, that's why they never told their children that they belonged to a royalty. They all were living a normal and simple life, just like everyone else in the town.

Both the girls were searching for Aravir and Sarath. When Sriha noticed Aravir and Sarath talking under the wide Banyan tree on their college campus, she nudged Ashmi with her hand and pointed towards the boys. Ashmi also turned around to see the boys and they both sprinted towards them. However, as soon as they heard the boys, Sriha and Ashmi were stunned and exchanged a look of disbelief.

The boys had no idea that the girls were standing behind them, listening to their conversation. They continued discussing,

"Last night, I had the same nightmare that I've been having for the past few nights. At first, I thought it was just a coincidence or maybe I needed to see a doctor, but I was mistaken!" Said Sarath.

"I don't know either. This is happening to me as well. So, I also told you about my scary dreams." Aravir appeared concerned.

"It's not just you two; we've all been through something similar for many nights." Aravir and Sarath immediately turned around when they heard Sriha's voice.

Aravir looked at Sriha by squinting his eyes just for the clarity, and he asked, "Blurred vision and…"

"Misty weather!" Ashmi completed his sentence.

They all were dumbfounded.

"Why didn't you tell me before, Ashmi? We are living in the same house, yet I've never known." Aravir questioned.

"Because I was not sure about it. By the way, you didn't mention it either. If you had, I wouldn't have been so surprised today." Ashmi responded.

"Okay fine!"

Sriha and Sarath exchanged glances. They had also not shared anything with each other

After that, Aravir turned towards Sriha and Sarath, "Did you guys know about each other's nightmares?"

Sriha and Sarath shook their heads in no. Aravir folded his arms across his chest and asked, "Do you want to ask anything to each other?"

"After seeing you two discussing dreams and being surprised like this, I don't feel inclined to ask anything." Sriha answered.

"Why?"

"Because if we do, our situations will be the same as yours. Our curiosity has waned now." Sarath said.

"Yes! We should concentrate on figuring out the cause of these nightmares." Sriha suggested.

They all agreed with Sriha, realizing that it was not just a mere coincidence. Something unusual was occurring among them. Each had their own theories. Some believed it was magic, while others thought it was a frightening situation. They were all attempting to understand this situation from various angles, yet none were successful in solving the mystery. Eventually, they got discouraged.

"So, what will we do now?" Sarath broke the silence, seeking an answer.

"I believe this nightmare might be linked to something in our lives. It seems like someone is trying to communicate with us." Ashmi shared her perspective on the nightmare.

"But how do we uncover the truth?" Sriha asked.

"Now there is only one way that can help us." Aravir responded.

"What's that?" Everyone asked together.

"Simply follow your dreams, as simple as that! We're left with no other option." Aravir stated, raising his shoulder.

"You're right! Until now, we've only been hearing the suffering cries of a man and a woman, along with that unclear vision and hazy weather. But now, we are all in this together, so perhaps our dreams will unfold more chapters of this mystery." Sarath said.

"Alright, but remember, not a single detail of this mystery should be shared outside our group until we've figured out the entire puzzle. Especially that running gossip queen shouldn't know anything about our nightmares. Otherwise, she will create a mess in the whole college about it." Ashmi explained and the group concurred.

"Okay then, until the night falls, let's finish our assignments. We can't let the nightmare interfere in our studies." Sriha said.

They nodded and left for their respective homes together.

TWO

THE POWERS

As the day unfolds, each of them were trying to focus on their work, but their dreams had captivated their attention. Sriha was sincere and the only one who was able to concentrate on her studies. However, Ashmi and Sarath never liked studying, so they had a great excuse to not complete their work. Aravir was very good at studies but was easily distracted by outside things and when he would find something new, he often used to immerse himself in the history and enigmas of it.

Their entire day passed like this.

"It was a very long day. Finally, the moment has arrived. I had been eagerly anticipating this moment. Now I just want to delve into my dream world." Aravir murmured and chuckled in excitement.

He was not afraid at all. In fact, he was enjoying every moment of this dream journey. The others were also in the same boat, but they had no idea what was going to happen with them. The secret of their entire life was hidden within these dreams.

All four went to bed and slept. As they drifted off to sleep, their dreams started flashing. And as Sarath had mentioned, this time actually they encountered something new. In their previous dream, they had seen foggy weather and a vision of a man and a woman crying. But from this dream, their real adventure, their actual journey was going to start.

This time, the fog started to move aside, revealing a clear path ahead. They were all amazed by the view. At that moment, they found themselves alone in different places.

Sriha stepped forward to witness the beauty of nature. As she moved forward, she felt that the speed of the wind was gradually increasing. Initially she was loving the cool breeze, but the rising wind flow was bothering her as it was getting more dangerous. She sensed something was off, but she could not do anything about it. Soon, the wind turned into a fierce tornado, sweeping Sriha along with it. She was frightened, but then, as she soared through the tornado, her fear dissipated, and she closed her eyes, raising her hands up. Then she was slowly lowering her hands. It seemed as though she knew how to calm the tornado. As soon as she lowered her hands, the tornado subsided. She landed safely and smoothly on the ground. After landing, she opened her eyes and realized she could control the wind. This was an astonishing revelation for her.

On the other hand, Anishiv found himself standing at the seashore. The gurgling sound of the water was soothing his heart. He was experiencing a unique kind of tranquility there. However, unexpectedly, he saw a massive wave was coming towards him. Anishiv was taken aback, unable to move backward due to the shock. And in a blink of an eye, the ocean engulfed him completely, as though the sea was attempting to swallow him whole. Anishiv shut his eyes in terror. Upon opening them again, he was still surrounded by water, yet surprisingly, the water didn't harm him. He was astounded by this revelation. He couldn't comprehend what was happening to him. Thus, he tried to touch the water. As soon as his finger touched the waster surface, the water started to recede. And he reached the seashore safely. He got confused and shocked at the same time. That incident left him utterly speechless.

Similarly, Sarath also encountered a similar ordeal. He was in the palace and strolling there. The palace was breathtakingly beautiful, and he was mesmerized by its beauty. While he was strolling in the palace, he felt as if something was burning. He looked around and spotted a burning curtain, which was ignited by a lamp near the window. The wind had blown the curtain into the lamp, causing it to catch fire. Gradually, the fire spread throughout the palace. He began searching for an exit from the palace. However, a burning pillar fell on him. Sarath thought he was going to die that day, but he survived, nothing happened to him. Half of his body was engulfed in flames, yet he didn't even feel any burning sensation. Somehow, he managed to remove the pillar from above him and stood up. He realized that fire couldn't harm him. He was still in disbelief, so he touched the burning pillar again, and the fire extinguished. He was shocked, so just to confirm again, he touched the pillar, he saw that the fire caught up again. He repeated this process two more times.

"I can generate and extinguish fire! This is incredible!" He started jumping with joy.

Next up was Ashmi. She was standing on the top of the mountain, mesmerized by the stunning sunset. Suddenly, she felt the earth beneath her began to tremble. Upon looking down, she noticed the mountain she stood on was on the brink of collapse. Some parts of the mountain had already started to crumble. And in a matter of seconds, she found herself tumbling down too. As she fell, she spotted a massive boulder hurtling towards her. Fear gripped her, and she extended her hand towards the boulder to shield herself. When she extended her hand, the boulder broke into pieces. She also crashed to the ground with a loud thud, suffering several injuries. While she was moaning in pain, her gaze shifted to the shattered pieces of the boulder, recalling the moment she realized a large boulder was on its way towards her as she fell from the mountain. She realized that something was strange. Soon after, she saw another boulder was coming towards her. She was unable to move because of her injuries. Uncertain of what to do, she remembered her previous action and immediately she extended her hand towards the boulder and this time kept her eyes open. To her surprise, the boulder shattered just like before. She looked at her hands, she had understood that she had the power to break anything.

All four were experiencing fantastic dreams, but as the night came to an end, their dreams broke, and they awoke. They quickly got out of bed and headed to their college after completing their daily chores. They gathered beneath the Banyan tree to discuss their dreams.

"I was caught in a tornado, but I have no idea how I managed to control the wind. Did any of you have the same dream last night?" Sriha asked.

"No, I was engulfed in a fire. Yet, I managed to put it out. The entire palace was engulfed in a massive fire, but as soon as I touched the flames with my hands, they were extinguished! I was able to extinguish the fire! Isn't that incredible?" Sarath exclaimed in awe.

"This is nothing compared to my dream. I was ensnared in a vast ocean wave. The wave almost consumed me, but I remained unharmed. As soon as I touched the water's surface, the high waves retreated." Anishiv shared his experience.

"What about you, Ashmi? What happened in your dream?" Sriha inquired.

"I was in a dire situation! I was on the brink of dying.

"I had tumbled down from the mountain and sustained injuries too. Then, I noticed a massive rock hurtling towards me. However, when I extended my hand towards the boulder to shield myself, it shattered into fragments. I was baffled by the power of my hand that could break such a large rock! Initially, I thought it might be a trick of the mind, so I attempted it again when another rock was about to strike me. The outcome was the same." Ashmi recounted her story.

Everyone was stunned by her story.

"But why do we have these kinds of dreams? What do they mean?" Ashmi pondered.

No one had an answer to their questions. However, these dreams seemed to have a connection to their lives. They discovered they could control different things in their dreams from the previous night.

This was giving them a clue about themselves. They were puzzled, thinking perhaps it was just natural. Whatever was happening to them was very surprising and new. They spent the majority of their day thinking over their dreams. They were all anticipating the night to continue their journey in their dreams, eager to discover what was next. As night descended, they had dinner and promptly went to sleep.

Their dreams resumed.

This time, they found themselves in a different location. The place was lush with greenery and adorned with vibrant flowers swaying in the gentle, cool wind. There was a trail paved with stones, fruits were dangling on the trees, and squirrels frolicking nearby. It was truly enchanting. Sriha began to walk on the path. As she moved forward, someone appeared from behind and scared her with a loud scream in her ear. She got scared and immediately covered her face, her heart racing. She then gently moved her finger from her face to see who had frightened her.

When she saw the person, she let out a startle, exclaiming, "You! What are you doing in my dream?"

Aravir burst into laughter, "Just look at your expression, how frightened you are!"

That person was none other than her best friend Aravir.

"I was scared, but now I'm angry. Why aren't you in your dream?" Sriha got irritated.

"Oh, come on Sriha! We all are experiencing the same dream, and we are in the same place as well. So obviously we will be in each other's dreams!"

"Is it really like that?"

"Absolutely!"

That brief exchange left Aravir deep in thought, realizing something profound. He mulled over it silently.

"What's going on? Is everything okay?" Sriha asked.

"It's quite peculiar! Typically, people don't realize they're in a dream. Yet, we're aware that we're living in a dream right now."

"You're right! But the situation we are in is equally odd. So, don't overthink it. Let the chips fall where they may." Sriha advised.

"By the way, it seems like a beautiful dream rather than a nightmare now." Aravir murmured, observing the surroundings.

"So, Sarath and Ashmi should be here too." Sriha scanned the area, hoping to spot them.

"Ya, they should be, but they might not be. Let's just hope they find us."

"By the way, Sriha, you look absolutely stunning! Like a princess! All our attire is different from real life." Aravir complimented, admiring her.

"Oh! I hadn't even noticed. I'm looking wonderful! My focus wasn't on my outfit." Sriha beamed at herself.

When she turned her attention back to him, she said, "Just look at your outfit, Aravir. It's as if you are a prince."

"I know! How could I miss that? I never forget to look at myself."

"Yes, of course! You're quite the self-obsessed guy! Now, let's go!"

They continued their journey, walking through the breathtaking scenery, a place that felt more like a magical realm. Both were enveloped in a sense of peace and joy.

"I don't think beauty like this exists in today's world. Modern life has stripped away nature's true splendor." Sriha commented.

While walking, they were both captivated by the view, as if they were absorbing the beauty of nature within themselves. They were relishing every moment of it. Suddenly, the kind of light caught their attention, and they saw that the light was emanating from behind the mountain. Both Aravir and Sriha exchanged excited glances. As soon as they moved forward, Sriha suddenly halted. She was unable to move forward, she felt as if her feet were glued to the ground, and she also heard the sound of something.

"What happened? Let's go. What are you waiting for?" Aravir asked.

"Aravir, can you hear something ringing? I think it's the sound of a bell." Sriha was trying to figure out where the sound was coming from.

"Bell!" he was confused. "I'm not hearing any kind of sound. Come on, Sriha, we have more stuff to explore." He said and started walking ahead.

But he felt no movement behind him. So, he turned around and saw that Sriha was still standing in the same spot.

"Why aren't you coming with me? What's wrong? Are you okay?"

"I can't walk, Aravir! It feels like my feet are frozen." She answered while trying to lift her feet.

"What? Let me check!"

As soon as Aravir walked towards her, Sriha suddenly disappeared. He was startled. He started looking his surroundings, but she was nowhere to be found. However, what actually happened was that she disappeared because her alarm had gone off and that's why she woke up.

Sriha let out a sigh, thinking perhaps Aravir was searching for her. On the other hand, in Aravir's dream, he was on a quest to find Sriha. But suddenly, he felt as though the ground beneath him was trembling. Upon looking down, he realized an earthquake had struck. He became extremely frightened and began screaming, which disrupted his sleep, and he woke up abruptly.

His heart raced, and he found himself gasping for air. He noticed his mom was pulling a heavy table. Then he understood that the sound of that drag had caused the earthquake in his dream. He breathed a sigh of relief. His mom noticed he was awake, she said,

"Oh! I'm so sorry, I disturbed your sleep. I urgently needed this table. Therefore, I came."

"It's okay mom! Let me help you."

After a while, he got ready and headed to college. As usual, they met on the college grounds, beneath the wide tree. That was their favourite spot. They used to spend a lot of time under that wide Banyan tree. It was a second home for them. Even during holidays, they used to jump over the wall and go under the Banyan tree.

"So, what's the news, guys?" Sarath asked, sitting under the shade of the Banyan tree.

"I and Aravir met in the dream. But I disappeared from our dream because my alarm went off. I thought you might be looking for me." Said Sriha.

"After you left, an earthquake hit my dream." Said Aravir.

"What? How?"

"My mom was dragging a table, so it felt like a massive earthquake in my dream. Dreams always seem like reality. I thought I was going to die. But later, my eyes opened."

That earthquake incident brought laughter to them all.

"Where were you both?" Sriha asked.

"I was also dreaming and exploring new places." Sarath answered with a smile.

Suddenly, Ashmi snapped at him, "Oh, shut up! You were busy eating fruits which were hanging on the tree."

That bright smile quickly disappeared from Sarath's face, and he retorted, "Ya, just like you were busy picking those colourful flowers, right?" he smirked.

Ashmi looked down, rolling her eyes in embarrassment. Aravir and Sriha were shocked to hear that. They exchanged glances.

"Guys, are you serious? We are trying to solve this puzzle here, and you two were just having fun there!" Aravir growled.

"But we can't control our dreams, it will come the way it would be. We can't do anything! We were just along for the ride." Sarath said, lifting his shoulders.

"True, we can't control our dreams, but we can steer our thoughts. If we keep our eyes on the prize, we won't get sidetracked by the distractions." Sriha explained in a calm manner.

They fell silent for a moment before they both said together,

"I'm sorry!"

"By the way, if you had not been distracted by other things, you would have seen what we have seen." Aravir said.

"What did you see?" Ashmi asked.

"We couldn't see much because our dream was interrupted. But we caught a glimpse of something shining behind the mountain." Sriha replied.

"We have not seen anything like that yet." Said Sarath.

"Alright, so we'll meet at a certain spot and then proceed. Aravir, please make sure you don't leave us behind." Ashmi instructed.

"But it's not in my hands to wait for you both!"

"But why?" Ashmi asked.

"As Sarath mentioned, we don't have control over our dreams. We can only meet when the time is right. We understand that we are dreaming, but that doesn't mean we can control our dreams." Aravir responded.

"But you and Sriha met each other in your dreams." Ashmi said.

"Yes, because there might be a reason for that. That's why we met. When your time comes, you will also meet us." Aravir said.

"So that means, we were not just having fun there, we were collecting flowers and fruits because we had been dragged by an invisible force! I was right, we can't control our dreams." Sarath said by raising his eyebrows.

Sriha rolled her eyes and said, "Alright, let's head back home. Another night is about to begin. Today, we've spent a lot of time together here."

Afterward, they all returned home and as usual, after finishing their daily chores, they settled into bed. They all drifted off to sleep, continuing their dream journey where it had left off. Sarath was munching on fruits, while Ashmi was contemplating what to do with the flowers she had gathered. Suddenly, she had an idea and placed a flower in her braided hair, making herself look elegant. Sarath and Ashmi were also in royal attire. Aravir and Sriha arrived at the spot where they had seen something shining. Ashmi and Sarath both moved forward. As they were coming from opposite directions, they unknowingly bumped into each other.

"Ouch! I'm sorry!" Ashmi said while rubbing her head.

"Ashmi! I'm so glad to see you!" Sarath exclaimed, happy to reunite with her. "Oh! So finally, we both met."

"It's great! I believe we have been split into teams. You and I, Aravir and Sriha." Said Ashmi.

"Yes, it's possible!" Sarath agreed.

"But it's odd that we can't control our dreams, yet we remember our discussions about our dream when we were awake," Sarath wondered.

"I don't know. It all seems to be a game of destiny."

Meanwhile, Aravir and Sriha moved forward to investigate the source of the light. However, they discovered it was behind a mountain, which meant they had to climb it to uncover its secrets. The climb was challenging, but they persevered.

As they ascended the mountain, they encountered many obstacles, but they didn't give up and continued their journey. Eventually, they reached the summit, where they were greeted by the first sight of the mysterious light. To their astonishment, it was not an ordinary thing or object, instead it was a magnificent royal palace, nestled in the middle of a lake, its brilliance rivaling that of a diamond. There was only a sailboat with oars that appeared at the lakeside. The sight of the palace left them speechless. The entire structure was constructed of glass, and the sunlight made it shine even more splendidly.

"Wow," Aravir said in hushed amazement with a wide open mouth.

"This is breathtaking! I have only seen palaces in fairy tale books, but those palaces are nothing in front of this one." Sriha was in awe.

"Would Sarath and Ashmi have seen this?" She asked.

"I don't know. We still haven't met them both. But why?" Aravir was wondering.

"Maybe, there would be a reason behind it." She thought.

On the other side, Sarath and Ashmi reached the mountain which was located at the opposite side of the mountain where Sriha and Aravir were standing. While Sarath and Ashmi were climbing on the mountain, they discovered a small treasure box that was locked and there was no key nearby. They searched for the key but couldn't find it anywhere. So, Sarath decided to keep the treasure box in his pocket and they continued.

When they both reached the top of the mountain, they saw the other side of the Glass Palace. They were also amazed to see the palace.

"It's magnificent!" Sarath said in wonder.

The reflection of the Glass Palace sparkled in their eyes. They were eager to explore the inside, yet their fascination with the palace was too strong to resist. All four were standing, slack-jawed and in awe at the tremendous size of the palace. As they were lost in the splendour of the Glass Palace, they didn't realize when the Sun ascended, and their dream came to an end.

It was time for them to go to college. They were all filled with anticipation to reunite and share their dreams. Because they had a lot of dreamy things to share. After that as expected they gathered at their favourite spot.

"Guys, you won't believe what we witnessed last night!" Sarath exclaimed, unaware that Sriha and Aravir had already experienced it all.

"We caught a glimpse of a massive royal Glass Palace from the summit of the mountain. It was so magnificent that words fail to capture its splendour. I have never seen a palace like this before." Ashmi expressed in awe.

Sriha and Aravir exchanged glances, caught off guard.

"Have both of you also seen the palace? Sriha asked.

When they heard Sriha's words, they understood that they all had seen the palace.

"It means we all have witnessed the grandeur and splendour of the palace. Amazing! So, there's no need for any more talk. We all understand that none of us can put into words the emotion we felt gazing at that magnificent palace." Aravir noted.

"But I couldn't spot you two anywhere on the mountain." Sriha inquired while squinting.

"We also didn't see you both!" Ashmi said.

"Perhaps, we were on a different mountain. There were countless mountains surrounding the palace." Sarath speculated.

"But we didn't come across any route to the palace. There was no bridge or boat." Sarath said while scratching his head.

"We did spot a boat by the lakeside." Sriha exclaimed quickly.

"Really? That's good! Now how will we find our way?" Ashmi said and gasped.

Out of the blue, Sarath recalled something and said, "We have stumbled upon something interesting."

"What?" Aravir and Sriha responded together.

"A tiny treasure chest, but it's locked." Ashmi revealed.

"Where did you keep that treasure chest?" Sriha inquired.

"In my pocket." Sarath answered.

"Excellent! Anyway, let's see what unfolds tonight." Sriha said, and they all headed back to their homes.

Once again, the evening descended, and they all succumbed to sleep. Their parents were puzzled, wondering why their children were going to bed so early these days. Yet, as the days passed, their curiosity grew stronger. The anticipation for the night ahead was building up in their hearts, as they were hoping to go into the palace.

In their subsequent dream...

They found themselves standing at the top of the mountain, with Sriha-Aravir on one side and Ashmi-Sarath on the other. Just like the previous night's dream, they were mesmerized by the beauty of the palace. Sriha was so captivated that she hardly blinked her eyes. Sarath was also lost in its beauty but all of a sudden, Sarath's attention went on the opposite side of the mountain. He squinted to see better and recognized the two figures. He nudged Ashmi.

"Look over there, Ashmi." He pointed out his finger towards the people standing on the other side of the mountain.

"If I'm not wrong, it seems they both are Sriha and Aravir."

Ashmi observed them carefully. When she also recognized them, she exclaimed in excitement, "Of course, they are Sriha and Aravir, you're right!"

She called out their names aloud, "Sriha! Aravir! Can you both hear me?" Her voice echoed across the land.

Sriha and Aravir heard a voice and immediately started looking around, but they found no one.

"The voice seems familiar, like someone we know called us." Aravir wondered.

Next, they heard another voice booming from afar, "Stop looking around, just look straight. We're exactly standing in the opposite direction from you both."

When Sriha and Aravir spotted them, they were overjoyed to find them at the top of the mountain.

"Hey Ashmi!" Sriha called out, waving her hand. "Let's go into the palace!"

"But how will we manage to enter the palace, there is no way." Sarath yelled.

"We can see a boat there. Both of you come closer to the palace and wait for us at the lakeshore." Aravir yelled too, to make sure Sarath and Ashmi could hear him.

"Okay, we'll wait for you. Come fast!" Ashmi shouted. All four walked ahead to their path.

Sriha and Aravir made their way down the mountain and reached the lakeshore of their side. They spotted a boat from a distance. The boat was tied to a tree nearby with a rope.

"If the boat is here, then someone must be here too." Aravir said while looking around.

"I don't think there will be anyone here. I haven't seen anyone since we arrived. We are alone here!"

"Maybe you're right! Let's untie the rope and row the boat ourselves. Oars are also there."

At that moment, they were about to untie the rope, but suddenly, the sound of someone yawning broke the silence. When they turned around to see, they saw an elderly gentleman who gradually stood up from the boat and stretched his arms towards the sky. The elderly man faced the palace, with his back turned to Sriha and Aravir. He had been asleep on the boat; therefore, Sriha and Aravir couldn't see him. The elderly man rested both his hands on his waist, and with hopeful eyes, he looked towards the palace. A range of emotions flickered in his eyes.

"I have no idea how long I'll have to wait," he murmured, exhaling heavily. "The palace is already glowing, but when will it truly light up?" he added, his voice tinged with a hint of sadness. Sriha and Aravir exchanged glances, puzzled by the old man's words.

"Excuse me!" Sriha called out, hoping to grab the old man's attention.

While the man was deeply engrossed in observing the palace with a kind gaze, he was startled by the sound of someone calling him in this deserted place. However, as soon as he heard the voice, he shifted his head slightly towards the direction of the sound. The man didn't turn his head completely, as he was doubtful about whether he had actually heard a voice. It seemed improbable to find anyone there. He even considered the possibility of it being a hallucination, so he gently shook his head to dismiss the thought and continued his observation of the palace. Sriha thought he might not have heard, so she called him once more,

"Excuse me, Sir!"

Then, he jerked his head slightly. His heartbeat increased. After a moment of contemplation, he still couldn't believe someone was calling him. Yet, the old man built up some courage to face the reality, he slowly turned around. The man had a long white beard and brown eyes, dressed in the attire of a villager.

When he saw two people standing in front of him, he couldn't believe his eyes. He rubbed his eyes and looked at them both again to ensure he was not dreaming. When he realized that they were actually standing there, the old man became extremely happy. His eyes became moist. He slightly smiled and blinked his eyes several times to hold back his tears.

"Hello sir! Can you please help us reach the palace?" Aravir asked with politeness.

The old man was totally caught up in the moment, but when he heard Aravir's voice, he snapped back to reality and said, "Sorry, I didn't hear. What did you say?"

"It's okay! Will you please help us to reach the palace?" Sriha asked.

"Of course! I'm here only to help you." He gestured to them to sit on the boat.

"Only to help us! What do you mean?" Aravir asked.

"A...Nothing! Just let's go. Come sit."

"But first, we need to pick up our friends from the lakeshore." Aravir pointed out his finger where Ashmi and Sarath were waiting for them.

"Sure! We'll get them."

They both grinned and settled into the boat. The old man took the helm and steered the boat.

THREE

THE MYSTERY

It was a new experience and a thrilling adventure for them. They were savouring every second of it. Their real journey was about to begin. It didn't matter; it was just a dream, because this dream was linked to the greatest reality of their existence. There were numerous mysteries they were oblivious to. This was not meant to be revealed to them in their dreams, as they needed to experience it firsthand to grasp the true essence of the situation, to understand the depth of the real situation. As their boat was moving towards the Glass Palace, their excitement was increasing. However, what else could they do? That Glass Palace was so captivating that anyone would get lost in its brilliance. Howbeit, the events unfolding around them were strange and marvellous itself, intertwined with their lives in ways they were unaware of. It is believed that what belongs to you will find its way to you. No matter how hard you try to prevent or achieve something, what belongs to you will come to you and what does not will not be obtained even after numerous tries.

The elderly man was keenly observing the excitement on the faces of Sriha and Aravir while sailing the boat. He was delighted to witness their enthusiasm. He had longed for this moment for years. The reason behind his anticipation and joy was still a mystery.

When Sriha caught the old man smiling while looking at them. She thought to strike up a conversation and introduce themselves to him.

"By the way, I'm Sriha and he is Aravir. What's your name?" Sriha asked.

"Mitral!" He responded while passing a gentle smile.

"Are you the only one here? Because we found no one here except you. Why is this place so empty?" Aravir asked.

"Because this place has especially been created for you all!" He responded in a whisper.

"What? I didn't understand." Aravir asked because he was unable to discern his words.

"A...nothing! I don't know why this place is so empty. But I have heard people saying that this is an abandoned place. So, I've come here because I don't want anyone to see me until I reunite with my lost ones"

Sriha and Aravir both were startled by his statement, and they were staring at him. Their faces were filled with confusion. Seeing their reactions, Mr. Mitral then explained,

"I mean, I'm alone here until my other buddies get freedom."

"Freedom from what?" Aravir asked.

"All of you will soon get to know once you step inside the palace." He answered and gently smiled.

Although they were still puzzled, they thought, "It's okay, let's just wait and see what unfolds."

Eventually, they reached the lakeshore where Ashmi and Sarath were waiting for them. After picking them both, the old man steered his boat towards the Glass Palace.

"Hello! Mr. I'm Sarath and this is Ashmi." Sarath introduced them.

"Hello, my name is Mitral! It's lovely to meet you both." The old man extended his hand.

"Hey, isn't it odd that he's the only one here?" Sarath whispered to Aravir, casting a wary glance at the old man.

"He has his own reasons. Don't worry, I have a gut feeling that he is a decent person." Aravir reassured.

The elderly man caught their hushed conversation but remained silent, he just passed an enigmatic grin and continued to steer the sailboat.

After a while, they arrived at the Glass Palace. disembarked from the sailboat and stood before the grand palace. They had spent initial few moments marvelling at its splendour. Eventually, they made their way to the entrance. It was a massive, ornate door that required collective effort to open. They all exerted their strength to open the massive door, and it swung open.

Upon stepping inside, their jaws dropped in astonishment at the sight of such a splendid creation. They could see their reflections in the walls, floor, and ceiling of the palace. It was crafted from glass that seemed transparent but was not. It was actually opaque. No one could see the person standing behind the glass barrier. Every nook and cranny of the palace was adorned with one-of-a-kind artworks from across the globe. There were candelabras placed at every table by each column.

All eyes were fixed on the palace, finding it amusing. However, Mr. Mitral was gazing at the palace with eyes filled with compassion and a kind smile.

"After so many years, I have stepped into this palace." He whispered, taking a deep breath, a look of contentment on his face. Tears welled up in his eyes.

Ashmi noticed Mr. Mitral becoming emotional and asked out of concern, "Mr. Mitral, are you alright?"

"Absolutely! I'm in a much better state now." He replied.

This response left Ashmi puzzled. "I'm sorry, I didn't quite get it. What do you mean by that?" She questioned.

"Relax! You'll all understand eventually. For now, let's just take a look at the palace." He suggested, ready to lead them inside.

However, he was about to take them all to explore the palace, but as expected, their peaceful slumber was once again disrupted by the alarm.

"Ah! I wish I could throw this alarm out." Ashmi expressed, hitting the alarm with the bed.

"But it's not the alarm's fault." She said, her voice became soft as she acknowledged it was beyond her control.

Subsequently, they all went to university and during their break, they gathered at their favourite spot in a circle, each one quiet, their eyes focused on each other's faces. After a while, Sarath couldn't hold it in any longer and asked,

"Who is Mr. Mitral?"

"Nobody knows the whole truth. So, it's pointless to talk about it, let's just see what unfolds ahead." Sriha responded.

"Let's hold off until tonight!" Aravir suggested.

"Agreed! By the way, I'm really looking forward to seeing the palace!" Ashmi exclaimed in excitement.

"You're right, it's like we are watching an entire movie in bits every night. The reason behind these dreams is still a mystery. Why are we experiencing this? I'm at my wit's end." Sriha expressed, taking a deep breath.

"I can't wait any longer." Sriha added.

"Neither can we. But what else can we do?" Said Aravir.

"Should we share with our parents?" Sarath suggested.

"No!" Sriha, Aravir and Ashmi all exclaimed in unison.

This sudden outburst scared him, making him stare at them with wide open eyes.

"Don't even think about telling them anything." Aravir cautioned him.

"But why?"

"They will be concerned for us. You know that we've made a firm decision not to share our dreams with our parents until we understand the true reason behind those dreams. Have you forgotten, Sarath?" Said Sriha.

"Relax! I was merely suggesting. I've kept it to myself. There's no need to worry!" Sarath responded in a composed manner.

"Everyone suddenly pounced on me." He grumbled under his breath.

"Did you say something?" Sriha asked while narrowing her eyes.

"No! I didn't!" Sarath stuttered while responding.

After discussing for some more time, they all left to their respective homes. As they departed, a person lurking behind the Banyan tree came out. It was Miss Sarati. Over the past few days, she had observed the four of them gathering under the Banyan tree daily, engaging in secretive conversations. So, this time she followed them and concealed herself behind the Banyan tree to eavesdrop on their entire conversation.

"The palace! It means, they have reached there." She mumbled.

While she was pondering over their discussions, suddenly her attention shifted to a hand of a girl, she was hiding behind the wall, with her back resting on it. That girl was completely oblivious to Miss Sarati's presence. Miss Sarati moved closer silently and stood beside her. When

Miss Sarati saw her face, she recognized the girl. It was Risha, the running gossip queen. Miss Sarati folded her arms across her chest. Upon seeing someone's shadow on the ground, Risha's heart raced with fear. She took a deep breath, feeling a shiver run down her spine, and looked beside her.

"What are you doing here, Risha?" Miss Sarati suspiciously asked.

Risha was frightened. She started to fumble, "I...I was just...waiting...for my friend. Just that. Nothing else." Before Miss Sarati could ask something further, she rushed away from there.

"I hope she hasn't heard anything." Miss Sarati worriedly mumbled.

On the other hand, Risha was panting. She mused, "Thank God! I was saved. I hope that Miss Sarati will consider my presence there as nothing more than a coincidence."

After a moment to compose herself, she began to piece together the discussion she overheard between Sarath and his buddies. They were discussing their reluctance to share their dreams with their parents.

"What kind of dreams are these? I recall that day, Sriha and Ashmi were also discussing their similar dreams. Why do they feel the need to conceal them from their parents?" Risha pondered.

"Regardless, I want to! I'll do it because I despise them. They've always been mean to me. I'll make sure they pay for it!" Risha exclaimed, flashing a wicked grin.

As the clock neared midnight, Sarath, Ashmi, Aravir, and Sriha hurried to their own rooms to sleep, so that their dream journey could start. Ashmi was a nightingale. She rarely went to bed early. However, over the last few days, she used to go to bed as soon as possible. This change caught her mother's attention, leading her to doubt Ashmi even more. But she had no clue about what was going on, so she chose to be silent.

Conversely, the four of them had entered into the world of their dreams. Mr. Mitral was taking them on a tour of the palace.

"This kind of palace can only exist in dreams." Sriha exclaimed in wonder.

"Indeed!" Ashmi concurred, gazing at the palace.

"This palace is real, and it does exist!" Mr. Mitral exclaimed.

"Really! Where is it?" Sarath asked with curiosity.

"Of course!"

"Have you been here before? It appears you are familiar with every detail of this palace." Aravir questioned with doubt.

"I'm your guide here. And that's all you need to know right now. You all gathered at the same place and met only me. Why? That's not a small coincidence." Mr. Mitral said.

"What do you mean by that, Mr. Mitral?" Sriha asked.

"Come with me!" Mr. Mitral said, leading the way.

They made their way into the grand hall of the royal court. This was the place where all the big decisions for the kingdom were made, and the king had the ultimate say in everything. As they entered the grand hall, their eyes were immediately drawn to two magnificent thrones. These thrones, crafted from crystals and adorned with valuable gems, sparkled in the light, captivating everyone's gaze. It was an enchanting sight for them.

"Wow!" They all were aghast.

Ashmi and Sarath made their way to the thrones and began to play the roles of the king and queen. After watching them like this, Mr. Mitral, Sriha, and Aravir couldn't help but laugh.

"Come on guys, let me take you all ahead." Mr. Mitral said.

He led them all into a secluded room. Mr. Mitral unlocked the door, and they all went in. They explored the space, examining everything with keen eyes. When Aravir and Sarath noticed the portraits on the wall, they were taken aback. At that moment, Sriha and Ashmi were busy looking at other things.

"Hey! Don't you think the person in that picture looks just like me?" Sarath asked Aravir, his eyes were locked on the photo.

"This looks exactly like me!" Aravir whispered in amazement.

Aravir was looking at another photo. Therefore, he didn't catch what Sarath was talking about. Upon receiving no reply from Aravir, he nudged him and repeated his question without moving his eyes from the portraits.

"Aravir, where are you lost?"

Aravir snapped back to reality and turned his attention towards Sarath. Sarath's eyes remained glued to the same photo. Aravir followed his gaze and got shocked too.

"You too!" Aravir exclaimed in surprise.

Upon hearing Aravir's statement, Sarath jerked his head towards him. He saw him staring at those two photographs over and over again. Thus, Sarath also looked at both pictures. After that, he too was left speechless.

Sriha and Ashmi also spotted similar portraits hanging on the wall. They were all surprised to see themselves in the photos.

Mr. Mitral noticed them engrossed in the portraits and looked shocked as well. He grinned at their surprised expressions. They were puzzled, so they turned their heads towards Mr. Mitral. However, his grin made them even more confused.

"Not only this, but there are also many more portraits hanging on that wall." Mr. Mitral said while pointing towards the other portraits hanging on another wall.

Upon hearing his statement, they started looking at those portraits carefully. The images left them astonished. In these portraits, they were adorned in regal clothing.

"Do you know about this, Mr. Mitral?" Sriha asked.

Mr. Mitral took a deep breath and moved a few steps closer towards the portraits hanging on the wall.

"Well! Of course I'm aware of this. That's precisely why I brought you all here." He responded.

Their confusion deepened by his words, intensifying their desire to delve into the history of those portraits. The four were eagerly awaiting Mr. Mitral's explanation, their gazes fixed on him. However, gradually their vision started getting blurred. Soon after a few seconds, the room plunged into darkness. When Sriha opened her eyes, she realized that it was time to pause their dreams, their dreams remained incomplete again. They all woke up from their deep slumber. Ashmi was exasperated by this pattern and said,

"Every time we are on the verge of discovering something new, the Moon disappears, and the Sun appears." She let out a frustrated sigh.

They would attend college, reunite, return home, and dream. This routine had become a part of their life. Yet, the mystery behind those dreams remained unsolved. However, they were hopeful that in their next dream, they would uncover the history behind those portraits, and they were very excited for that.

Sriha, Aravir, Sarath and Ashmi were sleeping peacefully. They found themselves face to face with Mr. Mitral. They were eager to know how he knew about the palace. The portraits increased their confusion more, prompting Ashmi to ask, "We are baffled, Mr. Mitral. How did our photos come here? We are visiting this palace for the first time! What's the significance of bringing us here?"

Mr. Mitral was cognizant of the myriads of questions swirling in their minds. So, he decided to reveal the truth.

"I understand you guys are confused and seeking answers. I will disclose everything, but for that you all have to be patient. Because I cannot tell you everything at once. All the secrets will be revealed one by one. So, for now, come with me." After making this promise, he started walking.

Everyone trailed him. He escorted them into the massive library, also located within the palace. This was another splendid locale that left all four in awe. They discovered that the study tables and chairs were made from glass and embellished with precious gems such as rubies and emeralds. The shelves held numerous books, each hiding its own enigmas. It was a moment of wonder for everyone.

"Please, take a seat, my children!" Mr. Mitral beckoned to the chairs arranged in a circle around the study table.

They all settled in. Mr. Mitral grabbed an ancient book from the shelf and joined them at the table. The book, 'Descendants of the Glass Palace', was sealed. Mr. Mitral glanced at Sarath.

"Hand me the treasure box." He said while extending his hand towards him.

Sarath was startled by how he knew about the treasure box. However, everything was already a mystery and confusing for him. So, he handed it over without questioning.

"Thank you!"

Mr. Mitral unlocked the treasure box with the key he wore around his neck, dangling from a chain. Inside the box, there was another key. He picked it up and unlocked the book. There was a photo of a royal couple. He turned the book towards them and showed them,

"The photo is of King Ashan and Queen Kauriya. Now turn the page, Ashmi!"

Ashmi followed his instructions and flipped the page. They saw another picture which was also of a royal couple, King Harishan and Queen Vedarsha.

"Who are these people and why are you showing it to us?" Sriha asked.

Mr. Mitral smiled and said, "Now get ready to find out the answers to all your queries. I'm going to unveil the truth behind your dreams, that is why you all are getting these dreams every night. Listen to me carefully. The story is intertwined with all of your lives."

They all leaned in, eager to hear the story. Mr. Mitral also took a deep breath and started to disclose the truth.

"You were all born into a royal lineage in your previous birth. Aravir and Ashmi were siblings and offspring of King Ashan and Queen Kauriya. In a similar vein, Sarath and Sriha were siblings and the children of King Harishan and Queen Vedarsha."

The group looked at Mr. Mitral with astonishment.

"Whenever your parents would meet, you all used to play together, and you all had formed a bond which was unbreakable. The portraits you saw on the wall, was of a moment you all had spent together that time." Mr. Mitral recounted their past life's narrative.

"The Kings had jointly constructed a palace as a testament to their genuine friendship and trust in one another. They both had an equal share in the palace. They aimed for it to be a unique and magnificent structure, unlike anything seen or heard of before. They hoped that the palace would serve as a symbol of their profound friendship. They wished for their children to grasp the essence of friendship and to cherish it. And the best part is that where we all are sitting right now, is the same palace that your parents had established, "The Glass palace!"

As soon as Mr. Mitral mentioned the name Glass Palace, it sent shivers down everyone's spines. The mere mention of 'Glass Palace' was enough to give them goosebumps.

"Really?" Sarath exclaimed with a loud voice.

"This is our palace, wow!" Ashmi was taken aback by Mr. Mitral's words.

"I can't believe this!" Sriha also mumbled underneath her breath.

"As you all can see, each and every thing in the Glass Palace is made of glass. The palace is transparent, but respecting everyone's privacy, they had built this palace in such a way that no one could see anything from one side to the other." Mr. Mitral explained.

"That's why we all had the same dream. Because we were all deeply intertwined in our past lives." Aravir wondered.

"That's true! But not only for this reason, there are other reasons too."

"There are more reasons! What?" Ashmi asked curiously.

"You'll find out soon. I'll reveal the full story" Everyone listened intently to Mr. Mitral.

"King Ashan and Queen Kauriya, the parents of Aravir and Ashmi, were living a prosperous life. The friendship between King Ashan and King Harishan was so deep that even other kingdoms appreciated their bond. But it is said that people have evil eyes on every good thing." Mr. Mitral paused for some time.

Aravir, Sriha, Sarath and Ashmi could sense that the dark side of the story was about to start. So, they also braced themselves for Mr. Mitral's commencement.

He proceeded after taking a deep breath,

"One day, King Ashan and King Harishan, along with their families, visited the Glass Palace to celebrate their triumph in battle. Their ministers and stewardesses were always used to being with them.

However, celebrations in the Glass Palace used to be extraordinary because of the beauty of the palace. After the festivities concluded, the kings and their queens retired to their chambers. Their children were playing in the courtyard, while the ministers of both kings stood on the balcony, clutching the railings.

Shangir, the minister of King Harishan was repeatedly rubbing his hand on the glass railing, which was gleaming, and his reflection was mirrored on it. Tushyan, who was the minister of King Ashan, observed this and chuckled.

"It's splendid, isn't it?" Tushyan remarked.

"Indeed, it's marvelous!" Shangir responded, his gaze fixed on the railing.

"Ah! The feeling of being in a Glass Palace, it's amazing!" Tushyan closed his eyes, savouring the moment.

Shangir looked at him and grinned. "You love the Glass Palace, right?"

"Who wouldn't? The thought of visiting the Glass Palace itself is a dream for many. Don't you love the Glass Palace?"

"Of course! I adore the Glass Palace! In fact, at times, I find myself dreaming of owning it. Being crowned as the King of the Glass Palace is a great honor."

"You can achieve that if you desire!"

"That's absurd! We are ministers, and the palace is already under the rule of our respective kings." Said Shangir.

"So what?"

Shangir turned his head towards Tushyan, adopting a serious expression as he asked,

"Is it possible?"

"Of course, if you don't let your desire die then everything is possible." Tushyan responded.

The desire to possess the Glass Palace had taken root in their souls. Both were intensely looking at each other. Shangir pondered for a moment and questioned once more,

"Would it be fair to betray our kings? They have placed their trust in us!"

"Nothing comes easily, you'll face both victories and defeats. If you let your emotions take over, you'll never succeed in becoming the King of the Glass Palace." Tushyan said.

Shangir's heart skipped a beat upon hearing the phrase 'the king of the Glass Palace'. He was instantly lost in deep contemplation.

"Don't think too much, my friend! Everything is fair in love and war. And this is war for the love of the Glass Palace." Tushyan smirked.

"But how is that possible?"

"Through careful strategy, we can both ascend to the throne of the Glass Palace and can achieve Kushalraj and Madhuraj too."

The thirst to own the king's properties was sparkling in their eyes. Their greed for wealth and authority was increasing. Tushyan also moved his hand on the glass railing and said,

"The Glass Palace, which symbolizes their friendship, will be the cause of their downfall." Tushyan burst into laughter. Shangir also passed a devilish smirk.

Aravir, Sarath, Sriha and Ashmi were shocked.

"Then what happened, Mr. Mitral?" As soon as Sarath asked, a dazzling light appeared from somewhere. He couldn't withstand the brightness, so he shut his eyes. After a few moments, upon opening his eyes, he found himself back in his bed. He understood that his dream had been broken. Sarath saw the sunlight because his mother had opened the curtains from the window, and the Sun rays directly hit him.

"Ah, not again!" Sarath groaned in frustration as his dream was shattered once more. The other three also woke up, feeling as though the day stretched out like an eternity. The wait of night seemed to grow more unbearable with each passing moment. However, they managed to convince themselves to endure it.

Meanwhile, Risha was set on carrying out her sinister plans. When she saw Aravir, Sriha Sarath and Ashmi conversing beneath a Banyan tree, she went to Sriha's house to spill the beans to her mother Srishtika. She knocked on the door and Srishtika opened it.

"Yes?" Srishtika asked, as she did not recognize her.

"Hello ma'am! I'm Sriha's friend, Aashruti." She pretended to be Sriha's friend so that Sriha's mother wouldn't doubt her, and She also fabricated her name, so that Sriha wouldn't discover who had informed her mother.

"Actually, I wanted a note from her for my project. Is she at home?"

"No, she has gone to college. Why didn't you borrow it from her in class?" Srishtika asked.

"She has not attended college today. So, I thought she's been plagued by nightmares or maybe she's sick. That's why I came here to collect her notes. As I need to submit my project tomorrow." Risha cleverly hinted to Sriha's mother about their nightmares.

Srishtika was taken aback by Risha's revelation. She asked with curiosity, "One moment, what did you say? Nightmares? About what?"

"Don't you know about her nightmares?" Risha pretended not to be aware that Sriha's mother was clueless about her nightmares. "Okay I'll tell you."

"Hold on!" Srishtika was concerned about not wanting anybody to eavesdrop on their conversation, so she directed her to come inside.

They settled onto the couch, and Srishtika said, "Now tell me everything you know. What's troubling her?"

"I've heard her discussing her nightmares with Ashmi. She mentioned seeing a man and woman weeping and pleading for their heritage's protection. What's more intriguing is that Ashmi, Sarath, Aravir and Sriha are all experiencing similar nightmares from the past nights."

Srishtika was not even blinking her eyes while listening to her. She was shocked as hell. She again eagerly asked,

"What else have they seen in their dreams?"

"I don't know much, but yesterday, they were talking about the palace, and they were excited to visit that palace."

As soon as Srishtika heard about the palace, she felt as if the ground beneath her feet shifted. Her heart skipped a beat. She was unable to say anything further. Risha noticed her stunned reactions and couldn't help but smirk. Then she decided to leave before Sriha returned home, so she quietly exited from Sriha's house, leaving Srishtika in a state of shock.

After coming outside of the house, she smirked and said, "Today, a bolt of lightning is going to strike them." She let out a loud laugh.

When college hours finished, Sriha made her way back home. She entered and turned around to shut the main door.

"Do you have something you need to share with me, Sriha?" Srishtika asked coldly.

Sriha was confused by her mother's sudden inquiry, so she slowly moved around and spotted her mother seated on a chair with a serious expression. Sriha felt a bit uneasy.

"Why are you suddenly asking this question?"

She smiled. "Nothing, just felt you look tense from the past few days, so I thought I'd check in." She answered in a courteous way, as though nothing had happened.

"No, there is nothing important that you need to know. There is no need to worry, mom!" Sriha reassured and hurried into her room. She settled on a bed and took a deep breath.

"Does she know anything?" She wondered. "No, no! She has not mentioned anything, so I don't need to worry."

When Srishtika shared this matter with her group. Parthan questioned,

"Why didn't you tell her that you have discovered the truth?"

"I believe it's not the appropriate time to bring this up. If we ask them anything about this matter, they will not reveal the entire truth. They will share only what they want to and try to hide many important secrets from us. So, it's better that we wait for them to disclose everything themselves, as we have already decided." Said Srishtika.

"You're right! Anyway, we can't stop what is happening, so let's just go with the flow. Maybe this is our destiny."

Anishiv added.

FOUR
THE TRUTH

A new dream had started. They were sitting in a vast library with Mr. Mitral. Sarath had asked him about what had happened ahead in the story. He answered,

"The rulers, King Ashan and King Harishan often used to visit the Glass Palace. Both the ministers were on a quest to discover a flaw in their respective rulers that might lead to the dissolution of their deep friendship and trust, however, each attempt ended in failure. They were fully cognizant that it was nearly impossible to fabricate or discover any incriminating evidence against their rulers and sever their connection, yet they persisted in their search. After a few days, when they grew weary, Shangir remarked,

"Our dream of owning the Glass Palace will remain just a dream. Their bond is too formidable, I don't think I would be able to break it."

"So, will you give up so easily?" Tushyan questioned, looking at him.

"But what other options do we have?"

"We have! If you can't find any fault in them, then falsely accuse them. It's as simple as that!"

"What do you mean?"

"I mean, I have a plan, which I am going to share with you. Listen to me carefully." Tushyan had devised a sinister plan which he shared with Shangir.

"Now do as per the planning. This time we will surely win." Tushyan said with confidence.

"What if we lose? There is a lot of risk."

"Then I might have to eliminate the ruler." Tushyan murmured.

Shangir couldn't understand his murmuring. He simply concurred with Tushyan's strategy and went back to his role as the minister of Madhuraj.

Kushalraj and Madhuraj were thriving and formidable realms. Kushalraj was ruled by King Ashan and Queen Kauriya. In a similar vein, Madhuraj was governed by King Harishan and Queen Vedarsha.

Shangir was greedy, but Tushyan was not just greedy; he was also malevolent. Shangir's only goal was to become the ruler of the Glass Palace. However, Tushyan aimed for more; he sought control over Kushalraj and Madhuraj as well. He manipulated Shangir for his nefarious ends, and Shangir was not as astute as Tushyan. He was oblivious to the fact that he had become a pawn in Tushyan's schemes.

For a few days, everything proceeded without a hitch, but then, out of nowhere, Tushyan disappeared. King Ashan and Queen Kauriya began a frantic search for him. However, he was nowhere to be found. They grew concerned for his well-being. Then, unexpectedly, King Ashan's troops stumbled upon Tushyan, lying unconscious in the middle of the street with numerous scratches and a bleeding head. They then brought him to Kushalraj. King Ashan was shocked by his minister's condition.

King quickly asked, "What happened to him?"

"We don't know, your majesty, we found him lying unconscious in the middle of the street." One of his soldiers answered.

The king started getting worried for him. He thought to let him regain consciousness, then he would ask him about the real matter.

After several hours, when Tushyan regained consciousness and slowly opened his eyes, king Ashan rushed to him and asked,

"What happened to you, minister? How did you end up in this state?"

"Our neighbouring sovereign had attacked me." Tushyan answered in a trembling voice.

"Which sovereign was it? We have three neighbours. Just tell me I will not leave them; they must face the consequences for their actions against my minister." King Ashan was enraged.

"Oh king, you will be shocked upon learning the name of the ruler who attacked me." The minister stated, his eyes were fixed on the king.

"Who is that king? Tell me his name!"

"His name is King Harishan!"

The king was rendered speechless upon hearing the name. He found it hard to believe.

"King Harishan! This is unfathomable! You must have been mistaken, minister. He is my closest friend; he could not do this!"

"I understood that you might not believe, but this is the reality, my lord!"

"How is that possible! They will never harm our kingdom. There is no motive for them to turn against me." The king stated.

"I know that King Harishan is your closest friend, but when people become overly ambitious, they can do anything to achieve their desires."

"What greed could it be? He is blessed with everything. He is even wealthier than me." He wondered.

"What had occurred during the attack? Tell me everything." The king asked.

"They attacked me because I overheard their conversation. They were planning to steal the Glass Palace which both of you kings have established together." The minister answered.

"But we both already own the Glass Palace, and we have an equal share in it."

"Indeed, but King Harishan wants complete ownership of the palace. He doesn't want you to have a share in it."

"Do you have any evidence? Without concrete proof, we cannot directly accuse him." King Ashan questioned.

"I don't have any proof right now. But I will make an effort to gather it if you allow. However, King Harishan is now aware that I know the whole truth, so he will likely attempt to conceal or safeguard their secret."

"But since they know that you overheard their entire conversation, why didn't they just end your life? They should have killed you." King Ashan asked suspiciously.

Tushyan got scared and just to hide his lie he stuttered and said, "They left no stone unturned to kill me, but I somehow managed to save my life and escaped from there. They had kidnapped me the day I learned about their conspiracy. Moreover, they wanted me to hide this secret from you. They attempted to persuade me and even bribed me. But when I declined to cooperate with them, they tried their best to end my life so that their secret would not reach you."

King Ashan was quiet. The minister's heartbeat increased as the king's silence filled the room. The minister was constantly staring at him while waiting for his reply. After a moment of contemplation, the king finally got convinced and said,

"Fine! You have my approval to proceed. Gather concrete and authentic proof against King Harishan. After a thorough inspection, I will proceed with my decision based on the evidence. But remember, Minister, if your accusations against my beloved friend are proven false, severe consequences will follow for you as well." He cautioned him.

The minister was frightened, yet he nodded in agreement. A few days later, once he had recovered, he began his investigation.

On the other side, every king used to have their own covert operatives (secret agents). King Ashan summoned his secret agent and instructed him,

"I can sense that something is wrong with the minister. My friend can never betray me. Hence, I instruct you to monitor the minister's every move, but remember, the minister must remain unaware of your surveillance. I will tell him that you are keeping an eye on King Harishan."

The secret agent agreed and went off to carry out the king's directive. Later, King Ashan told his minister,

"I have appointed a secret agent to keep an eye on King Harishan."

As soon as Tushyan heard about a secret agent, he became frightened. King could see the sudden shift in his demeanour.

"There is no need to appoint any secret agent, king! I'm already working on it." Tushyan said hastily.

"It's okay! I know you are already working on it. But if a secret agent will be there to help you, we will get strong evidence against King Harishan quickly."

Tushyan got silent. his fear was evident on his face. King Ashan could see his unease.

"What's making you so anxious? Don't you want the secret agent's help?"

"No, it's not like that. It's good that you appointed him. You're right, I will get help. Thank you!" Said Tushyan with a forced smile to the king.

King Ashan's doubt was gradually increasing. But he chose to remain silent until the truth came out. He was sure that Tushyan would definitely try to harm him after learning about the secret agent who was on a mission to find out the truth, so that whatever plan he had made would not be compromised. Thus, he had recruited an additional secret agent, and Tushyan was unaware about him. The king thought that the first secret agent would divert the minister's attention, in the meantime, the second secret agent would find out the whole truth and get the accurate information to him.

The next day, when King Ashan was seated in his private chamber, his second secret agent came to him.

"My lord, King Harishan is innocent. He has not committed any wrongdoings. The minister is deceiving you. I may not understand the exact motive behind his falsehood, but I will soon discover it and report back to you." The secret agent stated and exited through the back entrance, ensuring the minister couldn't intercept or capture him.

"I knew that! My friend can never betray me. I trust him more than myself." King mumbled.

Subsequently, he called the first secret agent and instructed him,

"Now listen to me carefully. You have to lie about King Harishan in front of the minister when you come to the courtroom."

The secret agent nodded and left. When he came out from King Ashan's private chamber, Tushyan blocked his way and stared at him.

"What information have you got about King Harishan?" Minister asked in a stern voice.

"The King has prohibited me from disclosing any information."

"I am the minister of King Ashan, and nothing is concealed from me."

"I have not discovered anything yet. King had summoned me to act swiftly." He answered so conveniently that the minister believed him and unblocked his way.

Tushyan thought that he could not harm the undercover agent until he discovered something, or else he would be accused by everyone. Therefore, he decided to wait until he found out the truth. Tushyan was merely observing him. As predicted by King Ashan, the minister got busy.

After some time, when the meeting started, the first secret agent came into the assembly hall. The minister was also sitting there.

"Oh king! King Harishan is really betraying you. He has also hatched a conspiracy against you." The agent made up this story as he and King Ashan had decided.

Tushyan was confused by the false allegations against King Harishan, because he knew that King Harishan was actually innocent. He had followed him earlier to see if he had discovered anything, but he had found no evidence.

"Why is he lying?" Tushyan wondered.

King Ashan was observing his expressions closely. He also acted as if he was hurt because of the betrayal of his dearest friend. He wanted to break the chain of his thoughts.

"I can't believe that my own friend can hoodwink me. My heart shattered into fragments." He let out a heavy sigh.

"You were right, minister! King Harishan has to pay for this." Said King Ashan.

Tushyan gave a slight smirk. He thought he won the first step. However, he was mistaken. Later, at night when King Ashan was sleeping, the minister tiptoed out of the palace. He didn't want anybody to know that he was going somewhere. The second secret operative caught him spying around, prompting him to follow him. The minister sneaked out of his kingdom and headed to Madhuraj (King Harishan's kingdom). The minister travelled to the hidden location of the kingdom, where another individual arrived to meet him. This spot was shrouded in darkness and was located underground. The secret agent was shocked when he saw the face of that person engaged in conversation with Tushyan. He turned out to be the minister of King Harishan, who was known as Shangir. The agent recognized him afar because they were carrying a lantern with them.

"Have you begun your task?" Tushyan inquired.

"I have commenced. And what about you?" Shangir responded.

The undercover agent was eavesdropping on their discussion from behind a large, imposing stone. Tushyan informed Shangir,

"King Ashan has already believed that King Harishan is plotting against him. You too have to stir up trouble. Your task is to induce poison into his ears and incite him against king Ashan, so that King Harishan would start to believe that King Ashan really wants to seize the Glass Palace."

Tushyan was unaware that King Ashan had sent his own secret agent to monitor his activities.

"Alright! I will take care of it." King Harishan's minister, Shangir responded with a smirk.

"We just have to sow the seed of doubt in their hearts. This small spark will turn into a huge fire. Then both of them will attack each other's kingdom and kill each other. Afterwards, both of us will be entitled to the Glass Palace," Said Tushyan.

The secret agent was dumbfounded by the revelation of their plot. He contemplated immediately alerting King Ashan to their scheme. However, as he was about to depart, he noticed both ministers (Tushyan and Shangir) exiting from the dark area. They were departing from different paths. The agent quickly concealed himself behind the large, imposing stone again. After a few steps, Tushyan halted. The secret operative got scared, suspecting that the minister might have realized someone was eavesdropping on their conversation. The minister stopped because a thought struck him. Shangir had already left the place.

"King Harishan is innocent, but why did the secret agent of King Ashan accuse King Harishan of treachery? Why did he deceive him? I'm aware he had no proof against King Harishan, so why did he fabricate such claims? I forgot to discuss this matter with Shangir also.' He wondered.

After thinking for a while, another thought popped into his mind. He smirked and mused,

"Perhaps he is also cunning like us and aiming for the Glass Palace or Shangir might have tricked or misled him to make our way easier. Therefore, he is also making up false stories and presenting in front of the king. Albeit, what can one do? The Glass Palace is such a beautiful palace that anyone's intentions can be spoiled." He chuckled.

"Oh, poor King Ashan! I feel pity for you. You are surrounded by cheaters. Only cheaters! How tragic!" He laughed and walked away.

The secret agent overheard his mumbling and quickly went to king Ashan after Tushyan left the place. He shared the entire conversation with king Ashan.

"Thank God, I got to know about reality. My strategy worked." King Ashan said and thanked the secret agent.

Afterwards, King Ashan was thinking about what to do now. His trusted minister had turned against him, just for the sake of the Glass Palace, which he and his dearest friend King Harishan had established together. However, that palace was so wonderful that anyone would be tempted to make it their own.

At such times, the distinction between oneself and another becomes apparent. As he mulled over these thoughts, one idea popped up in his mind and he wrote something on a piece of paper and scrolled it. Then, he called his second secret agent again and instructed him,

"Now, listen to me carefully. Deliver this letter to King Harishan and instruct him to read it in solitude." He handed over the scrolled letter to the secret agent. The agent nodded and headed to fulfill King Ashan's command. After some time, he arrived at Madhuraj, and once the councilor's meeting concluded. He made his way directly to King Harishan's private quarters.

"Oh King! Your dearest friend King Ashan has sent you a letter and has advised you to read it when you're alone. Make sure nobody should be around you." The secret agent informed and departed from the kingdom.

King Harishan was confused by his friend's request to read the letter in private.

"What could this letter contain? I am curious." He thought.

He opened the letter. The letter was,

"Dear King Harishan,

I hope you and your family are in good health and spirits. I have to send this letter in private because I wanted to alert you. Our minister's intentions regarding the Glass Palace have been spoiled. They are betraying us. If we won't take any actions against them right now, they will ruin everything. I am unable to disclose all the details in this letter. Therefore, I request that we should arrange a meeting in disguise, making sure our ministers are unaware of our disguised meeting.

Your dear friend,

King Ashan."

Upon receiving this letter, the initial thought that crossed his mind was that it might be a forgery or sent by one of his adversaries to deceive him. However, upon closer inspection, he noticed a hidden emblem on the letter. This emblem was known only to King Harishan and King Ashan, marking it as their secret sign. This revelation put his doubts to rest. King Harishan found it difficult to believe that his own minister would act in such a manner. Yet, he trusted his friend's integrity and decided to meet him to address the matter thoroughly.

King Harishan donned the guise of a destitute man and went out of his kingdom without informing anyone in the kingdom. To ensure his safety, he placed pillows beneath a sheet and instructed his doorkeepers to prevent any visitors from entering. He said,

"In case anyone persists, inform them the king is preoccupied with some crucial matters and prefers solitude." Subsequently, he made his way to meet King

Ashan.

King Ashan did the same, he disguised himself as a poor man and stepped out of his domain to meet King Harishan. After a while, they both met at the lakeside, which was centrally located between Kushalraj and Madhuraj.

"How are you, my friend? It's been quite some time since our last meeting." King Ashan asked. They both embraced each other.

"I'm doing well. How about you, my friend?" He responded.

"Terrible news, my friend! The ones we placed our trust in have turned against us. Our advisors are planning to pilfer our Glass palace, which we built for our offspring and as a tribute to our genuine friendship." King Ashan answered anxiously.

"But I find it hard to believe that my advisor could do such a thing!" King Harishan exclaimed.

"I can understand your feelings at the moment. I'm also experiencing similar emotions. I'm not making any accusations without solid proof. When I learned about my minister's sudden disappearance, I had sent my troops in search for him, and they discovered him unconscious on the street of Kushalraj in a critical state. I asked about the reason behind his condition, so one of my soldiers mentioned your name as the reason."

"I was the reason! I don't know anything about it! I have no idea!" King Harishan was shocked.

"I know, my friend! You can never harm me and my kingdom. My minister informed me that you were discussing with someone that you want the entire share of the Glass Palace."

After hearing this, King Harishan looked at king Ashan in disbelief.

"My minister also mentioned that he was present at that time, overhearing your entire conversation, and you caught him and attempted to kill him. So, he can't inform me."

"I have no knowledge of this situation, Ashan!"

While placing his hand on King Harishan's shoulder, he said, "I trust you, Harishan! Thus, I had sent my covert operatives to keep an eye on him and his every activity. After that I found out the real face of the minister, I realized the situation was far from what he had led me to believe. He was spreading a deceitful narrative to provoke me against you."

"But this is hard for me to accept." King Harishan was confused.

"I understand your confusion, my friend! Thus, I urge you to trust in this matter only after thorough investigation, just as I did. Investigate this matter the way you want. Once you get entirely convinced about their malevolent plans, we shall reconvene here."

King Harishan concurred with his words and returned to his kingdom.

Days went by, King Harishan was observing Shangir's every move yet found no evidence of wrongdoing. Everything seemed perfect to him. So, he resolved to meet King Ashan and clear out King Ashan's misconception. Upon exiting his chamber, he noticed his minister Shangir, looking around as though he was trying to sneak out from the palace silently. King Harishan thought,

"It seems as though God has given me this great opportunity to dispel all my uncertainties."

King Harishan trailed behind him. Tushyan and Shangir reunited at their usual spot. They were exchanging updates with each other about the progress in their conspiracy. King Harishan got a reality check about his minister's malevolent intentions. His temper was on the verge of erupting like a volcano, but somehow, he managed to control his anger and left from that place. Later, King Harishan sent a message to King Ashan through his secret agent, notifying King Ashan to meet him at the banks of the same lake. King Ashan also left without delay to rendezvous with King Harishan.

"I apologize, my friend! I didn't trust you." King Harishan confessed.

"It's not your fault, Harishan! My situation was equally bad as yours. It's okay!"

"So, what should we do now?" King Harishan asked.

"They both are hatching a conspiracy against both of us. We will do the same!"

"What do you mean?"

"We will also ensnare them in their own conspiracy. Now listen to me carefully, my friend! Your minister will also come to you and will try to put poison in your ears against me. But you don't need to say anything. Just feign shock and you trust your minister. This will lead them to believe we are both ensnared in their scheme.

This is how they both will think that we both have been trapped into their game. After that, when the right time comes, we will roll our dice."

King Harishan nodded in agreement, "Alright then, we'll reconvene once my advisor takes the next move."

Subsequently, they both returned to their respective realms. As King Ashan had mentioned, King Harishan's advisor arrived and began to administer poison to his ears against King Ashan. Shangir also appeared before King Harishan in the same condition as Tushyan. He was wounded, with a bleeding hand and a cut on the corner of his head, multiple scratches all over his body, and struggling to walk. Observing his condition, King Harishan asked the reason behind his bad state.

"Oh King! Your beloved friend King Ashan is betraying you. He is planning to seize the Glass Palace from you." He responded in a trembling voice.

The King remained silent for a while, but later he thought that his minister would doubt him. So, he pretended to be shocked.

"How could he betray me? I will not leave him." Harishan portrayed himself as furious.

King Harishan didn't want his minister to suspect him, therefore he treated him as if he was genuinely hurt and angry. Following these events, both the Kings met once more, disguising themselves as impoverished men.

"Hmm!" The ruler stood by the lake where their initial encounter had taken place. He let out a sigh and remarked,

"You were correct! I had treated him as if he were my own brother, yet he turned against me solely for the sake of material gain." He lightly shook his head and inhaled deeply. His eyes were wet. He was concealing his inner turmoil.

"A kingdom whose minister is both wise and trustworthy, is a wealthy realm. Our ministers were wise but lacked integrity and loyalty to us and our realm. I had never anticipated such behavior from them! It's deeply distressing for me."

Tushyan and Shangir remained faithful to them until the establishment of the Glass Palace. Thus, King Ashan and King Harishan were taken aback by the betrayal of their own ministers. They could not even imagine that. This betrayal was particularly painful to them.

Then, King Ashan placed a hand on his friend's shoulder, attempting to offer comfort, "I understand, my friend, but we must not lose our courage. We need to defend our realm against this conspiracy. They are both vying for control of the Glass Palace and desire to dominate over other realms. We should be thankful to God that we found out the truth on time."

"You're right!"

King Harishan took a deep breath and declared, "Soon I will launch an attack on your kingdom."

King Ashan nodded and responded, "According to their plan, we will both attack each other, but then we both know what to do."

They both smiled and embraced each other warmly. Subsequently, the monarchs headed back to their own realms. Tushyan, unable to find any deceitful evidence against the kings, advised Shangir to poison King Harishan's ears and at the same time warned King Ashan, saying,

"Oh King! They are quite cunning. They are preventing me from gathering any evidence. I think they are aware that we know about their conspiracy. We must act swiftly, otherwise they can also attack our kingdom."

King Ashan pondered over this for a moment and said, "You're right, it seems now is the opportune moment to act."

A few days later, both monarchs prepared for conflict. As they had decided earlier to engage in a battle, they arranged their chariots, horses, elephants, and a vast army. They were poised to confront each other's territories. Shangir and Tushyan were elated to see the monarchs gearing up for war. They proudly climbed into their chariots; their minds filled with visions of triumph. However, they were oblivious to the trap awaiting them within their own schemes.

After a while, King Ashan and King Harishan arrived at the battlefield with their forces. Standing face to face, they exchanged a polite smile. Shangir was already envisioning a fierce battle, with both monarchs ultimately meeting their demise.

"Finally, I turned their friendship into a rivalry. I will soon be the sole ruler of the Glass Palace." Tushyan mused, a sly grin spreading across his face.

In the same breath, Shangir was also contemplating the same. In short, they were plotting to sever a robust alliance between the Kings, so that both the kings would destroy each other, thereby creating an opportunity for the ministers to take over the entire realm and the Glass Palace as well.

Tushyan was more devious than Shangir, though Shangir was equally cunning but lacked wisdom. Tushyan menacingly fixed his gaze on Shangir and mused,

"After the death of King Ashan and King Harishan, I will also eliminate Shangir on this same battlefield. Because I don't want to share my wealth with anyone." He smirked.

After surveying all the combatants on the battlefield for a moment, the two kings signalled their charioteers to converge. It was only King Ashan and King Harishan moving forward, as they had instructed their troops to maintain their positions until further notice.

When King Ashan and King Harishan reached the middle of the battlefield, both of them dismounted from their chariots, looked at each other and gave a gentle smirk.

Shangir and Tushyan were staring at both the Kings by narrowing their eyes. They were curious to witness the intense war between two best friends.

"Today is the most fortunate day for me, as the dynasty of King Ashan and King Harishan is going to end forever. It will be the dawn of my dynasty's rule over the kingdom and the Glass Palace." Tushyan thought with a chuckle.

In the midst of battle, the two monarchs were standing face to face, but neither of them was preparing to strike. Ministers were waiting for a declaration of war, but the kings were only looking at each other. Tushyan was growing increasingly agitated and struggled to maintain his composure, but he couldn't stop himself and eventually blurted out,

"Oh King, what thoughts are crossing your mind? He has deceived you; your loyal companion has turned against you. Why aren't you taking action? What are you waiting for?"

King Ashan inhaled a deep breath and turned towards his minister, who was waiting for his response.

"You said that my friend has betrayed me, right? And I should confront him. Okay then!" King Ashan said, turning back to King Harishan. He extended his arms and gave a slight nod. King Harishan comprehended his gesture and went to him.

They embraced each other. Both the ministers were shocked by this unexpected turn of events. They found themselves utterly perplexed by the situation.

After seeing them both in each other's arms, Shangir couldn't contain his reaction and exclaimed, "Your Majesty! How can you be with him? He is your adversary, yet you are embracing him!"

"Just look at us, minister. This is the essence of true friendship. True friends never betray one another, they never question, they only have faith. No one can sever our unbreakable bond." King Harishan stated, with a sense of pride towards King Ashan.

Both of the ministers were shocked and scared at the same time. They were getting angry as well. Their minds were a whirlwind of complex emotions.

"What were you thinking? We'll believe the baseless tale you concocted, huh!" King Harishan shouted.

"Do you think we are idiots? I did not receive this kingdom as a present. I have earned this throne. And I know how to safeguard my subjects, this kingdom and the throne. That is why I am the ruler, Minister." King Ashan said in a loud voice.

"What did both of you think, you would conspire behind our back, and we wouldn't even know? We staged this phony conflict merely to demonstrate the strength of our unity." King Harishan clarified.

The ministers' pride was wounded. Tushyan sharply protested, "You shouldn't have to do this to us."

Shangir also stepped forward and said, "We're not going to let you off so easily. Just wait and watch!" After making that statement, he unsheathed his sword from its sheath. As soon as he did, the king's troops surrounded and caged the ministers from all directions.

"You can't do anything. You have lost your game." King Ashan said.

"Commander, throw them behind the bars. And bring them tomorrow morning into the council hall. I will say what punishment they deserve." King Harishan ordered his commander.

"I never believed our ministers could turn on us, especially those we considered loyal. And now, for the sake of material gains, they've lost it all. Greed is a terrible thing." King Harishan sighed.

"But I'm pleased that another's trap failed to shatter our bond. Because we have faith in each other, and we are loyal as well." King Ashan expressed with a soft grin.

"We got freedom from someone's trap. It's time to rejoice today. What do you say?"

King Ashan raised his eyebrows and answered, "That sounds like a great plan! Let's go, but where do we go? I want to celebrate our victory out of my kingdom."

"Then it's obvious, the Glass Palace! It represents our friendship. And today our friendship has triumphed, we should celebrate there. What could be better than the Glass Palace!" King Harishan proposed.

"Oh yeah! That would be the perfect place! We will go tomorrow with our whole family."

"Done. See you tomorrow. I'll directly reach the Glass Palace."

Both the Kings were happy, but on the other hand, ministers were hell angry with whatever had happened to them. Shangir and Tushyan were locked up in separate cells.

"You've done wrong, King Ashan. I swear, I won't leave you. I'll make your life hell. I had struggled so much to become your minister. No one was willing to make me a King. Therefore, I became the prime minister and planned everything to achieve my goals. But you snatched everything from me." Tushyan was thinking while sitting behind the bars and sighed in frustration. Anger was clearly visible in his eyes.

His line of reasoning was interrupted by the dialogue taking place among two guards positioned outside the prison. "I wish to see King Ashan. My family is in distress. I will request King Ashan. He will surely help me." One of the guards expressed his worry.

"But he's not going to be here today." Another guard responded.

"Why?"

"Because he has gone to spend some time with his family. And King Harishan has also accompanied him with his full family."

"Okay! But where have they gone?"

"They have gone to the Glass Palace."

Upon overhearing their discussions, Tushyan had a thought and smirked. Perhaps he was planning something evil. Following that, the minister began to act as though he was ill. His body was trembling, and he let out cries as though he was in severe agony. The guards heard his cries and turned their attention towards the cell, where they found Tushyan lying on the floor, shivering as well. For a few moments both the guards looked at each other and then to the minister with the suspected eyes. They were at a loss for what to do.

Tushyan was aware that gaining their trust wouldn't be easy, so he feigned extreme distress. A guard was scrutinizing him closely. The minister's convincing demeanour persuaded the guard to help him. He could not see him suffering. So, he shook his head and said,

"We must take him to the doctor, come fast!"

"But how can we trust him? What if he's deceiving us?" The second guard protested, halting the first.

"I don't think so! Just look at him, he's suffering from so much pain. We can't be so cruel like him." The first guard argued.

After thinking for a while, the second guard agreed to take him to the doctor. They unlocked the cell.

As soon as they unlocked the cell and stepped inside, the minister attacked the guards. He was formidable, skilled in combat and he also knew how to use weapons. He was also a trained warrior. But he had no weapons to defend himself and escape from the jail. So, he started punching them and grabbed a sword from one of the guards. All the guards collapsed, and they were injured too.

Tushyan came out from his cell and helped Shangir escape as well. They managed to break free from the prison and immediately headed to the Glass Palace, where the Kings and their families were in the midst of a celebration. Upon arriving at the Glass Palace, they observed the soldiers were strategically placed throughout the area. Therefore, they slipped into the Glass Palace from the rear. However, the entire Glass Palace was guarded by a massive force of soldiers, so the ministers were stealthily moving forward. Following this, Tushyan and Shangir both positioned themselves behind the soldiers who were standing near the door. The ministers covered their mouths to prevent them from making noise and twisted their necks, causing the immediate death of the two soldiers. Subsequently, they took off their own clothes and dressed in the uniforms of the deceased soldiers to blend in with the others and also to steal their weapons.

After that, the ministers began eliminating the guards one by one. One of the guards spotted them and realised they were too strong to be stopped, so the guard made his way into the palace and approached the Kings directly.

"Your Majesty! The ministers have infiltrated the Glass Palace and are slaughtering our soldiers mercilessly!"

The Kings were taken aback and exchanged glances with each other in shock.

"But how did they manage to get here? They were locked up, weren't they?" King Ashan fretted.

"I'm not sure how they managed to break free, but they're both on their way to kill you all." The guard responded with worry.

"We need to act quickly. Guards, hurry! Stop them and bring them here." King Harishan commanded his other guards.

The soldiers encircled the ministers. They all pounced on the ministers. Tushyan and Shangir also confronted them. Gradually, the troops overpowered the ministers. Eventually, Tushyan realized that he couldn't kill such a big army alone. He was not able to defeat them. So, he surrendered, and the guards captured both of them and took them before the King.

"Minister, how did you manage to escape from the prison?" King Ashan asked angrily.

The minister responded, "What were you hoping for, I would remain imprisoned in your dungeon? Never!"

"But now you are in our cage, minister. Don't forget that!" King Harishan said with a smirk.

"Guards throw them both behind the bars. We will hang them tomorrow morning. This is the sole penalty you both deserve." King Ashan decreed.

The guards proceeded to carry out the king's command. They dragged the ministers along with them, as the ministers were not ready to go with them.

'I won't give up; I will surely kill them. It doesn't matter how I do it.' Tushyan mumbled to himself.

While the soldiers were dragging them. Tushyan spotted a soldier's knife holster. He quickly snatched a knife from his ankle holster and stabbed a guard in the stomach, then sprinted towards the king. The king, too, drew his sword and began to duel with him. Both kings instructed their families to keep their distance from them.

They all began to clash. Up until that point, Shangir was trapped in a cage of two other soldiers, so he struck his elbow into the soldiers' stomachs and pushed them. Then, he quietly took a sword that was lying next to the soldier's corpse and plunged it into King Harishan's abdomen. To this point, no one had noticed the altercation. However, as the king began to wince in pain, the attention of everyone present shifted towards him. They were taken aback by the severity of the king's condition. His family erupted into screams and rushed to his side, their cries echoing loudly. King Ashan also rushed to him and swiftly removed the sword from his abdomen. At that moment, Tushyan seized the opportunity to do the same as Shangir, stabbing King Ashan from behind. The king collapsed. That horrifying moment left them all in shock. Both kings had been attacked by their own ministers. The children of the kings were both terrified and enraged. They began to assault the ministers with their feeble punches. However, the ministers were so brutal that they showed no mercy towards the children as well. They lifted them up and threw them aside.

King Ashan was incensed and somehow managed to stand up to the minister to confront him. The minister, frightened by the king's bravery, backed away. King Ashan took off the sword from his back and thrust it into the stomach of Tushyan. King Ashan then said,

"I know your offspring will emulate your path and will attempt to strive to seize the Glass Palace, but I curse you that you and your descendants will never be able to rule over the Glass Palace. Your progeny might manage to take over our kingdom Madhuraj and Kushalraj temporarily, but they will fail to conquer the Glass Palace. Because the core of the Glass Palace is bound by the power of friendship, a concept you people don't even know about. The light or radiance of the Glass Palace will scorch people like you upon their approach. This perilous light will decrease only at the arrival of the real descendants of the Glass Palace."

After saying this, they both collapsed. Tushyan died. King Ashan knew that the peril was not fully vanquished. Shangir was still alive, engaged in the slaughter of other soldiers. King Harishan was also suffering from immense pain.

Afterwards, Shangir approached Queen Kauriya. She was frightened, but to protect herself and her children, she wielded a knife against the Shangir. The Minister sustained a hand injury, which only fueled Shangir's anger. His eyes turned a deep red. He grabbed Queen Kauriya's hair and tossed her into the water from the palace's window. Queen Vedarsha realized that the situation had spiralled out of control. Thus, she instructed all the children to flee from the palace and save their lives.

"Listen to me carefully, my children. The circumstances are deteriorating fast. It seems there is no chance to save ourselves from this disaster. But I want my children to be saved. The minister is currently engaged in a conflict with the troops. You all must escape from here as soon as possible. Save your lives, my children." She placed her hand on their heads.

"No mom, how can I leave you here alone. We will not go without you. You're coming with us." Sriha said while crying.

"Yes mom, we won't go alone. You have to come with us. Moreover, where shall we go? Who will look after us without you?" Aravir asked.

"No, my child, I cannot accompany you. I must prevent the minister from chasing you all. From now on, all you have is, each other's support, you all have to take care of each other and yourself as well. Above all, always remember one thing, my children. Just like your fathers and your family, always trust each other, shun treachery, and be benevolent. The bond between King Ashan and King Harishan was deep and unbreakable, that's why those ministers couldn't make them apart from each other.

Additionally, both the Kings have ascended to heaven together." Queen Vedarsha paused; her eyes filled with compassion as she looked upon her children.

"Now just go and preserve our legacy. I don't want our heritage to perish." Her voice quivered with the ache. It was incredibly hard for her to part ways with the pieces of her heart. Elsewhere, what other choice did she have?

In the midst of this intense conversation, Queen Vedarsha noticed Shangir coming towards them. She quickly moved the children out of the council hall and came back to stop Shangir. The minister was seething with rage, so he pushed her hard towards the pillar. The hard push caused her head to collide with the pillar and it started bleeding. As a result, she died.

Shangir surveyed his surroundings and thought he was the sole survivor in the whole palace. However, King Harishan was still breathing. When he saw that the minister had slain his Queen, he was overwhelmed with sorrow, the pain was too great to bear. He was furious and his fury propelled him to confront the vengeful minister. Thus, he grasped the knife and dragged himself towards Shangir. Somehow, he managed to stand behind Shangir. Shangir sensed someone's presence behind him. As he turned to face the person, in a blink of an eye, King Harishan pounced on him, stabbing him with a knife. Shangir also met his end instantly.

Harishan, the king, was on the brink of death. In his final moments, he gazed at his surroundings with a look of resignation.

"All have perished! Is this the end of my dynasty?" He whispered, his voice shaking, and fell on both of his knees, overwhelmed with grief.

The offspring of both kings rushed to his side. The king was on the verge of collapsing, but the children lifted his head onto their laps, tears streaming down their faces.

"No, King Harishan! The four foundational pillars of your dynasty are still alive." Anishiv spoke, his voice choked with emotion.

Upon hearing this, the king felt a sense of calm wash over him, and with eyes filled with hope, he said, "Then make a promise to me, my children, that you will preserve our dynasty and safeguard our legacy, our Glass Palace, which stands as a testament to our enduring friendship and the deep trust we place in one another." He made the request while extending his hand.

The four children clasped King Harishan's hand, promising to uphold his legacy.

"Don't worry, Your Majesty, we will protect this Glass palace. It doesn't matter how many years it takes to fight for it. We won't give up and will return with renewed vigor."

King Harishan was content and felt reassured by the unwavering determination in the young ones' spirits. His eyes welled up with tears. He was unable to utter another word, so he breathed his last.

Flashback ends.

"Everything was finished!" Mr. Mitral exclaimed. His eyes were sparkling because of the tears.

Aravir, Sriha, Ashmi, and Sarath were speechless, their eyes were also moist. This was their final night, their last night of dreaming.

After hearing the entire story, for a few moments, there was a pin drop silence. However, the story was still incomplete. A question formed in Sriha's mind, prompting her to ask Mr. Mitral,

"But what happened after that? Where have we gone? Did we die? Otherwise, how can we be here now?"

"All of you ran away." He answered.

"We ran away! Where?"

"I'm not sure about that." Mr. Mitral responded, averting his eyes from them.

"We must have died. Otherwise, how could we have been reborn?" Sriha questioned.

"I understand there are numerous doubts swirling in all of your minds, but for the time being, that's all you need to know."

They were confused. A sense of unease lingered, they felt that something was wrong, but at that time, nothing was in their hands.

"Our mission is to protect the Glass Palace, right? But who are our adversaries? After all, so much time has elapsed. No one is here." Sarath asked.

"Who claims no one is here?" Mr. Mitral questioned, eliciting a look of confusion from the group.

"The minister Shangir and Tushyan also have offspring and grandchildren. They will soon come and try to be entitled to the Glass Palace. And if it happens, you all will lose the Glass Palace forever!"

Silence enveloped them. Mr. Mitral took a deep breath, intending to leave, but again stopped to inform them something without turning.

"One last piece of information: from now on, your dreams will cease to exist."

All four children were perplexed as well as worried about if they won't have these dreams anymore then how would they be able to figure out what would be the next move they have to take to protect the Glass Palace? Sarath, unable to contain his calm, asked,

"How do we manage to save the Glass Palace? How will we foresee the next actions necessary for this endeavour?"

"Don't worry, Children! The Universe has conspired to align all things. There's no need for any action from your side." He assured them.

Though bewildered, they nevertheless concurred with his words. Mr. Mitral disappeared, signalling the end of their dreams.

FIVE

THE GLASS PALACE

The next morning, as they woke up and sat on their beds, the glimpses of the previous night's dream began to appear before them. All the dreams were roaming in their mind. However, after a while, they managed to shake off these thoughts and headed to college. They were seated in their classroom. Miss Sarati also arrived there.

"Our college has organized a trip." Miss Sarati announced.

"Where are we going?" Inquired one of the students.

"That's a surprise! We have heard a lot about that place. It's quite fascinating! It is saying that that place is very unique and has buried many mysteries in it, which have still been unsolved." Miss Sarati replied.

After Miss Sarati talked about the place where they were going for a trip, Sriha and Ashmi got confused, they even exchanged looks with each other. Miss Sarati was paying close attention to their facial expressions.

"Where could this place be? And what could it be?" Ashmi wondered and she was perplexed.

Their anxious expressions brought a smile to Miss Sarati's face, as she had been eagerly anticipating this moment for years. She intentionally made the situation more intriguing, hoping to witness their confusion and the transformation in their expressions, which she found delightful.

'This moment is the perfect opportunity for me to perform my duty as the prime stewardess of Queen Vedarsha and demonstrate my devotion to her.' Miss Sarati pondered and slightly smiled. The memory of Queen Vedarsha stirred feelings of nostalgia within her, causing her eyes to well up with tears.

Yes, Miss Sarati was none other than but the prime stewardess of Queen Vedarsha. She was also an important part of the whole mystery. This is why she was eager to learn about the conversation the two girls had earlier. She was going to be the medium to bring the four children to a place where they had actually belonged, and which was their actual home.

"We'll depart tomorrow morning at 5:30 AM. Be ready!" Miss Sarati said while looking at the two girls.

Sarath and Aravir were in a different class than Ashmi and Sriha. They both were also informed about the trip. They hadn't seen each other since their final dream. However, this time, they had thought to rendezvous at Sriha's house rather than beneath the Banyan tree of their college.

After returning from the college, the four of them convened at Sriha's residence. They were all dissatisfied with the fact that they had fled in their previous birth and didn't even know what happened with them ahead.

"But the mystery is still unsolved. Had we died or survived? And if we survived, how can we be present in this new birth?" Sriha was getting frustrated.

"You're absolutely right, Sriha! Perhaps Mr. Mitral was hiding something from us. He seems to be reluctant to disclose the outcome of our end in previous birth." Said Aravir.

"Now we won't even be able to see anything in dreams also. Because we won't have any dreams regarding this matter from now on." Ashmi expressed her concern. "I have no idea what to do now!"

"Relax, everyone! Remember what Mr. Mitral had mentioned, the universe itself will assist us. Somehow, we will undoubtedly make it to the Glass Palace." Aravir offered reassurance.

As soon as Sriha's mother, Srishtika, heard about the Glass Palace while she was passing by Sriha's room, she rushed in and inquired with curiosity,

"Glass Palace! Who's going to the Glass Palace?"

Sriha and her friends were frightened by her unexpected arrival and were also puzzled by Srishtika's inquisitive nature. Thus, Sriha inquired,

"Mom, why are you so curious? Do you know anything about the Glass Palace?"

"First off, who's planning to visit the Glass Palace?" She demanded in a serious tone.

The four of them were a bit scared by her stern voice. Consequently, Ashmi quickly blurted out, "We are going to the Glass Palace."

"Why?" Sriha's mother questioned.

They all exchanged glances with each other, contemplating whether to share their dreams with her or not?

"I already know about your nightmares, so don't even think about lying. Just tell me the whole matter." Sriha's mother almost yelled.

Sriha was shocked to learn her mother knew about their dreams. She also recalled the time when Srishtika had probed her. Sriha pondered,

"That's why she asked me if I was concealing something from her. But how did she find out about our nightmares?"

"Tell me what's wrong!"

Sriha realized her mother was upset and there was no use in making up stories. So, she chose to share everything with her.

"Alright, mom! We'll tell you everything, just sit down."

Her mother took a deep breath to calm herself and settled onto the bed. Afterward, each of the four of them began to share their dreams one by one.

She was paying close attention to every detail. Srishtika was dumbfounded by what she heard. Her heart started beating fast. The glimpses of her own dream of King Harishan started flashing in front of her eyes, where he had mentioned that her children will see their parents' past in their dreams as their previous life. And that's exactly what was happening to them. Srishtika was speechless, so without uttering a single word from her mouth, she quickly left the room to call Anishiv, Parthan, and Aparvi. She asked them to come over to her house as soon as possible.

After a while, the four of them met at Srishtika's house. The kids were in the bedroom, and their parents were in the living area. Just like before, Anishiv, Aparvi, and Parthan were observing Srishtika's worried expression.

"My dream was actually true! Our kids know about our past now." Said Srishtika.

They were shocked. Parthan, with a startling tone, inquired, "Have they discovered that those children were us?"

"No, they don't know about this yet. As king Harishan said, they saw our past as their own previous life." Srishtika answered.

"Don't you think we should reveal the whole truth to them?" Aparvi said solemned.

"Absolutely not!" Srishtika retorted firmly. "We must keep this a secret. You're aware of how perilous the minister's offspring can be." She scolded.

"But now we cannot stop our children. Do you really think that our children will remain quiet even after learning about the whole truth?"

"Exactly! Royal blood is flowing in their veins. They are not going to stop. If you try to stop them, they will find another way to reach the Glass Palace. Therefore, it's wise to reveal everything to them." Anishiv interjected.

"What do you wish to disclose to us, Dad?" Aravir asked.

They were shocked to see all four children standing behind them.

Sriha suspiciously asked them, "What's the truth? Please tell us everything. Mr. Mitral was also concealing something from us. How can we escape from the Glass Palace? I can't digest this!" Then Sriha shifted her gaze towards her dad. "If you won't tell us, we will discover the whole truth ourselves." She asserted.

Sriha's words compelled her father to confess the truth, fearing that if she discovered her own path to the Glass Palace, it would be more perilous. Therefore, he signed everyone with his eyes that they should tell everything to their children.

"Alright, we'll disclose everything to you all." Parthan stated.

"Mr. Mitral has already told you the truth that all of you ran away from the palace. But there was only one thing which was incorrect." He elucidated.

"What was that?" Aravir curiously asked.

"The four children you all saw in your dreams were not you four, but..." He paused, unsure of how to share the truth.

"But?"

"Those four children were us." He revealed.

Children were dumbstruck by this revelation. They were unable to believe it. They were taken aback.

"How is that possible? In our dream we saw that it was our previous birth's story. We were living our previous life." said Ashmi.

"Because I didn't want all of you to find out that those four kids were actually us. In fact, I didn't even want you to find out anything about the history of the Glass Palace, fearing it would endanger all of your lives." While taking a pause Srishtika smirked a bit and went on, "Howbeit, look at the game of destiny. Despite our best efforts, we couldn't prevent you all from finding out the history of the Glass Palace. you all eventually discovered the truth. We couldn't keep it hidden."

"We fled the Glass Palace, believing that once we had amassed enough strength, we could confront them. At that time, we were just little kids. That's why we had to escape. That was the only choice we had. So, we did what was necessary at that time." Srishtika shared.

"So, why didn't you go back to the Glass Palace?" Sarath asked.

"Because the Glass Palace is currently in the possession of the Tushyan's descendants. Moreover, not just the Glass Palace but the entire realms of both the monarchs is under their control." Aparvi responded.

"Kushalraj and Madhuraj?" Sriha asked.

"Yes! We had attempted to seek help from the inhabitants of that realm. But they refused to help us. Because they were also scared. No one was ready to even utter a single word against them. It had become exceedingly challenging to stay there, thus we were compelled to depart from the kingdom." Anishiv said.

"There was no one in the world whom we could call our loved ones except us four! We four were the only hope of each other. So, we decided to remain united. Later, we tied the knot and after a few years, you four entered into our lives. The moment we held four of you in our arms and embraced you all, we experienced a profound change. That feeling is unfeasible to express! That day we felt immense happiness as well as fear. We were stubborn to fight against the Minister's children before all of you were born. But after all of your birth, the fear of losing our children arose in my heart. Hence, I forbade Aparvi, Anishiv and Parthan from revealing the truth in front of all of you." Srishtika wept while talking.

"Albeit, now I have understood that if something is written, it will happen, and I can't defeat destiny. I made every possible effort to keep the Glass Palace's secret hidden from you all, but I couldn't succeed. The destiny itself wanted my children to

get involved in this mystery and so it is. The outcome is clear." She added and then turned around to bring the photo of her royal lineage from the hidden cupboard of her room. She carefully held the photograph and while compassionately looking at the photo, she said,

"My love for my children blinded me. I had neglected to consider the consequences that this would harm my own clan. Thus, now I'm determined to reclaim what had been taken from us." Srishtika said with firm resolve.

A gentle smile spread across everyone's faces.

"Thank you, mom!" Sriha exclaimed. Her heart was filled with gratitude.

"But you mentioned that those four children were not us, but you four. Then, how could they resemble us so much?" Aravir asked.

Parthan smiled and said, "We are your biological parents, and you are our offspring, so it's obvious that we will resemble each other."

"But there is something that still confuses me!" Said Sarath.

"What is it?" Parthan asked.

"The man who came in my dream was King Harishan, but who could be that woman who was crying?"

Upon hearing his statement, they began to ponder over it. However, Aparvi recalled something. During the attack on the Glass Palace, when Tushyan was troubling them, Queen Vedarsha made them run out of the palace. Aparvi realized that the woman the children encountered in their dream was none other than Queen Vedarsha.

She smiled and said, "She was your grandmother, Queen Vedarsha!"

"How can you be so sure?" Parthan asked.

"Do you remember the time when everyone was on the brink of death due to Tushyan's unexpected attack on the Glass Palace? She had saved us and told us to come back to save our heritage." Aparvi responded.

They all remembered that fateful day and nodded in agreement. And then there was no room for doubt, thus, they became united in this mission. They had resolved to reclaim their kingdoms and the Glass Palace, no matter the cost.

"By the way, tomorrow morning we are going on a trip." Said Aravir.

"Trip? Where?" His dad asked.

"I don't know! Teacher said that it's a surprise!"

"Alright then! Enjoy your trip guys." Said Anishiv.

"But what about the Glass Palace? I mean what will we do now?" Sriha asked.

"We'll discuss it later." Srishtika replied. The children concurred with her and left.

Next Morning, when they reached the college, Miss Sarati spotted them clustered together. She went to them and said,

"Come on guys, hurry up! We are running behind schedule. Please, go and take your seats on the bus."

They nodded and boarded the bus. The bus was all set to go. Aravir and Sriha occupied seats next to each other, while Sarath and Ashmi sat behind Sriha and Aravir. The destination was unknown to them, so they simply relished the journey. All were playing, singing and eating snacks. When they got tired playing and singing, they dozed off for a bit.

After five hours, they reached their destination. All were disembarking from the bus. From those four friends Sarath descended the stairs of the bus first. He was coming out by stretching his arms. When he completely got off from the bus, he looked left and right, putting his hands on his waist to see the place. But as soon as his eyes met with the view exactly in front of him, he froze. Sarath's eyes were wide open. Aravir noticed him in that position. He followed Sarath's gaze, which led him to the same spot. He was stunned too after seeing the view. The other two girls also came and after watching the scene, they both were also in shock. All four were astonished. What would they have witnessed?

They were standing in front of a huge and beautiful palace. And the most interesting thing was that, that palace was the same palace which they had seen in their dreams. That was the grand Glass Palace. While they were busy looking at the beauty of the Glass Palace, Miss Sarati tenderly gazed at them with teary eyes.

"I was merely a stewardess of Queen Vedarsha. Yet, she treated me as her closest friend. She considered me as her loved one. People who are generous and optimistic always leave their legacy behind even if they die." She thought and as she looked up, she closed her eyes in remembrance of Queen Vedarsha.

"I can feel your presence, Queen Vedarsha. That time you were my God. I needed you and you supported me through all my ups and downs, now I know, and I even understand your reliance on me, and I won't leave any single chance to do anything I can for your dynasty. I promise you, Queen Vedarsha." She gently opened her eyes, and a single tear rolled down her cheek.

She wiped out her tears and went to the kids who were still captivated by the splendour of the Glass Palace.

"Hello!" She waved her hand in front of their eyes as they were not in their senses. Despite this, they couldn't sense her presence.

"Hey!" She exclaimed loudly while snapping her finger in front of their faces.

Suddenly, they all came into their senses. When they saw Miss Sarati standing before them, Sriha pointed towards the palace and exclaimed,

"This...!"

Before she could finish her sentence, Miss Sarati interrupted, "The Glass Palace!"

"Why did we come here? I mean nobody lives here." Asked Sriha.

"Yeah, you're right! Nobody lives here, that's why the Glass Palace is the centre of attraction!" She answered.

Her facial movements and the sparkle in her eyes caught their attention. The manner in which she was talking, Sriha and her friends found it odd. They were exchanging glances amongst themselves.

"Ma'am, do you know anything about the palace?" Aravir asked suspiciously.

"Of course!" Miss Sarati responded while she was lost in her thoughts. The children's eyes widened, but soon Miss Sarati realized her mistake and began to stutter.

"I...I mean, no way! Absolutely not! How would I know anything about this palace? I had only recently learned about it, so I thought of visiting it." She fibbed to hide the secret and quickly moved away.

"Okay, if you're saying this, then it's fine!" Said Aravir.

Afterwards, Miss Sarati led them to the shore of the lake. As the Glass Palace was located at the centre of the lake. Therefore, they had to go through the boat. As the four had seen in their dreams, they had also seen a sailboat at the shore. Ashmi speculated that Mr. Mitral might be on the sailboat, so she ran to the sailboat and peered inside, but to her disappointment, it was empty. She gave a slight, disappointed look at her companions. Miss Sarati directed all the students to board the boat, so that they could go to the Glass Palace. Students did as she instructed them. Together, Miss Sarati and another teacher rowed the boat using oars. After approximately 30 minutes, they arrived at the Glass Palace. They disembarked from the sailboat and stood before the pristine and huge entrance. This sight brought back memories for Sriha, Sarath, Ashmi, and

Aravir of their dreams. Miss Sarati, along with them four, pushed it to open the massive door and stepped into the Glass Palace. As they navigated through the palace, each step brought back memories of their dreams. Miss Sarati, with her eyes filled with tears and a soft smile on her lips, looking around her.

Everything was just like their dreams. Infact, the actual experience was even more breathtaking and reminiscent for them. Miss Sarati had been away from the Glass Palace for so long that she became completely absorbed in it, unaware that her own tears were starting to flow. Her mind was filled with past memories, and she was so immersed in the moment that she could even see the Queen Vedarsha, King Harishan and their children giggling and playing around.

Aravir caught her becoming emotional and was confused with her behaviour. He felt sorry for her and at the same time he was getting suspicious too. Aravir went to Sriha and gently leaned in to tell her something,

"Don't you think Miss Sarati is hiding something from us?"

"Why do you think so?" She asked.

They both were standing behind her at a little distance, with their backs facing Miss Sarati. Aravir made Sriha turn towards Miss Sarati.

"Just look at her! Why is she sobbing? And the way she is behaving and looking at the Glass Palace is weird! It seems like she knows everything just like Mr. Mitral. I don't know why, but there is something fishy." He remarked while narrowing his eyes.

Coincidentally, Miss Sarati noticed them both staring at her. At that moment, she realized she was in tears. She quickly turned around, wiped out her tears and tried to appear composed. Sriha and Aravir also felt alarmed when Miss Sarati noticed their stares. They, too, turned around, trying to act as though they hadn't noticed anything; everything was normal.

"Is Miss Sarati a new teacher?" Sriha questioned.

"Yaa, she joined our college a few months back." Aravir answered.

"That's why we haven't really gotten to know her well," she pondered. "Don't fret! If she's up to something, we'll soon discover it."

At the same time, the other students were enchanted by the mystical charm of the Glass Palace. It was an unforgettable experience for all. Miss Sarati had noticed Aravir's growing suspicion towards her. Thus, she made up her mind,

"Tonight, I'll tell them everything. This is the perfect moment to reveal our secret, and we are at the right place as well. But before I spill any beans, I need to finish the most important work. And that's something that can only be done tonight, when everyone's asleep."

On the other hand, Aravir also laid out his plan to his friends. He declared,

"Tonight, we will find out everything. We are in the Glass Palace guys! We will surely find out something big, so that we can get an idea about how we can acquire the Glass Palace." He was enthusiastic.

"What if we're caught?" Sarath asked.

"Relax, at night everyone will be asleep. They won't even suspect us."

The four of them were clueless about Miss Sarati's plans, but Miss Sarati knew the four kids would probably try to uncover her secrets.

Therefore, she had planned to introduce them to someone who was very important, and the interesting fact was that they had already encountered him in their dreams.

As night fell, all the students went into their respective allotted rooms. The Glass Palace sprawled across a vast area, housing numerous rooms. Miss Sarati thought that the students might feel frightened being alone in their rooms, so she suggested that two kids would share each room.

Sriha-Ashmi and Sarath-Aravir's rooms were next to each other. They went to their rooms, because they didn't want anyone to find out about their plan. As the night deepened, and all were asleep, Sriha, Aravir, Sarath and Ashmi tiptoed out of their rooms.

"I hope we didn't get caught." Sarath wondered while looking around him to ensure no one was keeping eyes on them.

When they stepped on the terrace, they were amazed. They stood near the glass railing of the terrace; they could see the panoramic view of the entire town. The terrace's vastness and elevation made the scene breathtakingly beautiful and captivating. That view was nothing short of magical, leaving them all spellbound. This was an experience they had never encountered before.

"We had never visited the terrace in our dreams. It's truly wonderful!" Ashmi exclaimed while inhaling a deep breath.

Everyone's eyes lit up with delight.

"If our grandparents had not been killed, we all would have been together today. Now it all makes sense what Mr. Mitral was saying. If both of the Kings and Queens would have been alive, this kingdom would be alive with laughter, joy and happiness." Aravir said intensely while looking at the view.

"But everything went wrong. The entire kingdom is desolate." Sriha added.

"Wait!" Sarath interrupted. "But where is Mr. Mitral?"

"Yes! After stepping into the Glass Palace, we completely lost track of him. He is very important. After all, it was him who introduced us to everything about the Glass Palace." Sriha exclaimed.

"He's probably here. Before we do anything else, we need to locate him." Aravir stated, and turned around to go in search of him. As he turned, he was almost about to take a step, but upon noticing someone at the entrance of the terrace, he stopped.

"Are you guys on the lookout for me?"

The other three also heard the voice and the voice seemed familiar to them. So, they immediately turned around to check. They were astonished and in disbelief at the same time. They were both amazed and pleased because the person who was standing in front of them was none other than Mr. Mitral. Furthermore, they were taken aback by the unexpected encounter, as they had never imagined meeting someone from their dreams in reality. It was no less than any wonder for them.

Upon seeing their surprised faces, Mr. Mitral grinned.

"Hello!" He exclaimed while waving his hand.

Sriha, Aravir, Ashmi, and Sarath's shocked looks transformed into beaming smiles of immense joy.

"Where have you been, Mr. Mitral?" Sriha asked curiously.

"We were about to go in search of you." Aravir said.

"I was just waiting for the right time." Mr. Mitral answered.

All were looking at him with confusion. Then Mr. Mitral extended his hand towards the entrance door of the terrace and said,

"Now you can come. The moment has arrived!"

The four also turned their heads in that direction. At that time, someone held the extended hand of Mr. Mitral. The children were eager to see who this person was. When that person slowly came out, they were left in awe. It was Miss Sarati, the stewardess for Queen Vedarsha. The kids' minds were brimming with countless questions, but due to a clash of multiple questions they were unable to ask.

"I sense you all have many questions for me. Please, feel free to ask. I am here to provide answers." Miss Sarati responded.

However, what questions could they possibly ask? They were flummoxed and speechless. Mr. Mitral realized they desired to ask but were unable to do so. Thus, he took the initiative.

"Let me introduce her to you all. She served as the stewardess for Queen Vedarsha. Just like me, she is also an important part of this whole mystery."

"Miss Sarati was the stewardess of Queen Vedarsha!" Sarath exclaimed in disbelief.

Miss Sarati said, "Yes! When King Harishan, King Ashan and their Queens died, their four children, that means your parents ran away from the kingdom. Because there was nothing left for them, we could understand that! I had hoped they would return once they were ready to confront the wicked descendants of the ministers. But I didn't know why they hadn't come. I continued to reside in the realm of King Harishan, awaiting your parents' return to liberate us from the clutches of the Minister's offspring. The Minister's children had become the king of that realm. The people of King Harishan were tolerating the terrible cruelty of this new tyrant. Yet, your parents didn't return. Eventually, my patience had run thin. That's when I made the decision to escape the Madhuraj kingdom and embarked on a quest to find your parents. Alas, they were nowhere to be found. I was deeply saddened by this. Afterwards, I went to the lakeside to find solace. It was there I encountered Mr. Mitral. He asked me the reason behind my frustration. So, I told him everything. Mr. Mitral Mr. Mitral listened intently and understood everything, then he told me about all you guys. He told me that King Harishan and King Ashan's children got married and also have their own children. Later, we both devised a plan."

"Plan! What plan?" Asked Ashmi.

"When King Harishan was taking his last breaths, your parents had promised him that they would not let their dynasty die. And I guess they must have tried also. But nothing happened. Many years had passed. We all knew that King Harishan's soul won't get peace until your parents fulfil their promise. Therefore, he appeared in my dreams and told me to reveal the whole truth to you all. He wanted me to bring his grandchildren into the Glass Palace. So that you guys can deeply feel and understand the essence of true friendship. Moreover, I knew I couldn't accomplish this task by myself. I needed assistance. That's when I noticed Miss Sarati who was sitting distressed at the lakeshore. I knew her already. So, I asked her for help and instructed her that she would have to go to their college as a teacher and when the right time comes, she has to bring all of you here. And I'm grateful to her that she fulfilled her duty." Said Mr. Mitral.

Miss Sarati slightly smiled. When she shifted her gaze towards the kids, she noticed a bewildered expression on Aravir's face. He seemed deeply lost in thoughts. Thus, Miss Sarati thought to ask about his perplexity.

"Aravir!"

Aravir turned his attention to her.

"Aravir! What's on your mind? Why are you looking so muddled?"

"Minister's children have forfeited two kingdoms, Kushalraj and Madhuraj. But why didn't they forfeit the Glass Palace?"

Upon hearing his question, Mr. Mitral and Miss Sarati looked at each other and passed a gentle smile. Aravir noticed their reaction and asked,

"What happened? Did I ask something wrong?"

"No! Your question is valid. However, as we had previously said, the Glass Palace stands as a symbol to genuine friendship. Therefore, anyone with malicious intent cannot gain possession of the Glass Palace. It's not merely an ordinary palace; it has transformed into an enchanted one due to the curse placed by King Ashan. Both the ministers, Tushyan and Shangir, were cheaters. And cheaters can never rule over the Glass Palace. They had attempted to acquire the throne of the palace, but as they sat on it, the enchanted throne immediately threw them tumbling to the floor. They were unable to utilize any of the palace's treasures. The glass's reflections felt like flames against their skin. They had become compelled to depart the palace at once. And now, the curse of King Ashan is intensifying, and it will only grow stronger over time. The Glass Palace permits only those with pure intentions and who values true friendship. Just like you four, four of you share an incredibly strong connection. You all can even risk your lives for one another. Therefore, the reflection of the Glass Palace seemed like a cool breeze on our body and felt like a fire on theirs. And there's another reason why you four were able to enter the Glass Palace without difficulty, despite the curse. The reason is that you all are the 'Descendants of the Glass Palace.'" Said Mr. Mitral.

"But why didn't you mention that the four kids in the story you shared with us weren't we four, but rather our own parents?" Sriha asked.

"Because King Harishan believed it was important that your parents disclose the truth on their own. Once I found out that your parents had already shared the truth, I promptly informed Mr. Mitral, and we both agreed to disclose additional information, ensuring we could tackle this challenge as a united front." Miss Sarati explained.

"Ah, I see! But perhaps our parents are unaware that we are currently in the Glass Palace." Ashmi mumbled.

Upon hearing Ashmi's conversation with herself, Miss Sarati reassured, "Don't fret! Your parents will soon become aware of this."

"That means we'll also have the chance to visit the other two kingdoms, correct?" Sarath nearly leaped with joy.

The remaining three children also fixed their gaze on Miss Sarati and Mr. Mitral, hoping for their approval. They both were also enjoying the kid's excitement. Mr. Mitral and Miss Sarati exchanged glances. They decided to pull their legs, so they nodded negatively. The children's faces, filled with excitement and joy, soon shifted to expressions of sadness. When they saw their upset faces, Mr. Mitral and Miss Sarati burst into laughter.

"Absolutely, everyone will have the chance to visit the remaining two realms. Kushalraj and Madhuraj are rightfully yours."

Upon Miss Sarati's affirmative response, there was a collective sigh of relief, and they began to leap with joyous anticipation.

"Now, rest well. We will leave for Kushalraj at the break of dawn tomorrow." Mr. Mitral advised.

They all nodded and went down from the terrace, retiring to their designated quarters and slept.

In the early hours of the morning, Sriha stretched her arms, signalling the start of a new day. Her mind was blank and fresh until suddenly she remembered that they were going to visit their grandfathers' kingdoms that day. Without a second thought, she jumped out of bed, rousing Ashmi, who was sleeping next to her. She placed her hand on Ashmi's shoulder and shook her, because Sriha knew that Ashmi was not so active enough to wake up at the sound of someone's voice.

"Ashmi, wake up! Today we are going to visit our grandfathers' kingdoms. I can't afford to be late because of you. Get up, night owl!" Sriha yelled.

Even though Ashmi was never an early riser, after hearing Sriha's words, she leaped out of bed right away. Her sleep disappeared in a second as if she had never slept. Sriha was astonished. Ashmi quickly made her way to the bathroom to get ready. Sriha also came out in her senses and got ready. Once they were ready, the two girls headed to the assembly hall, where they had planned to gather. Sarath and Aravir joined them there. They were dressed in a way that made them look like ordinary villagers, similar to the locals of the kingdom they were travelling to at that moment. They opted for this look because they knew that Tushyan's son was the ruler of Kushalraj. They wanted to keep their real identity a secret.

"Are you ready, guys?" Miss Sarati asked.

"Absolutely!" they all agreed in harmony.

"Let's go then!" Mr. Mitral exclaimed, and they all hopped onto the horse-cart.

Only Aravir, Sarath, Ashmi, and Sriha accompanied Miss Sarati and Mr. Mitral. The rest of the students and teachers were oblivious to their plan. After a while, they arrived at Kushalraj, the realm of King Ashan. Once that kingdom was considered to be the most developed and prosperous kingdom and now when the four children saw that kingdom, it was in the worst condition. When they observed people of that realm, fatigue was clearly visible on their faces. Miss Sarati felt a deep ache in her heart witnessing the suffering of the populace. There was a period when they used to be the happiest people, this kingdom was full of compassion and happiness, but now it was a stark contrast. The eyes of the people were begging for help.

Earlier all the inhabitants of the kingdom used to be the children of the king. The king used to consider them as his own children and addressed their every concern. The sorrow and pain of the people used to be the sorrow of the king. They used to reside in the soul of the king. But when Kushalraj came under the possession of Tushyan's son, everything got ruined.

"The citizens of this realm seem to be in a state of deep sorrow. I'm feeling sorry for them." Sriha expressed with a heavy heart.

"What's the point of staying in this realm? Why don't they break free from their confines?" Sarath wondered aloud.

"The monarch has made it mandatory for them to reside here. He refuses to release them. Tushyan's son is acutely aware that the monarch's power is derived from his people. Therefore, he keeps everyone here forcefully so that they work for him. And poverty is another reason for their living here. They have no accommodation anywhere else. Here, they receive sustenance and shelter. It's different thing that they have to endure king's torture, but they have no other choice."

Everyone felt sorry for it. Miss Sarati surveyed her surroundings, her eyes welled up with tears.

"What kind of kingdom it has become. Earlier this empire was flourishing with happiness, but now it has withered." She closed her eyes and turned around.

"I can't see the kingdom like this! Once it used to be my home, but now I can't recognize this place. I want to leave this place." A tear rolled down her cheek.

Mr. Mitral could sense her distress. So, he gently placed his hand on Miss Sarati's head to console her.

"Have patience! Everything will be alright, if..." Mr. Mitral paused mid-sentence, then turned to face the children.

"If?" Aravir asked.

"If you all desire, this kingdom can be in a better condition. We brought you all here to witness the present state of the kingdom. To truly comprehend another's suffering, you must experience it yourself. I aimed for each of you to feel your people's hardships. Such feelings will stir affection for your subjects within your hearts."

Although, that's what was happening at that time. Subsequently, they made their way to Madhuraj, the realm of King Harishan. The condition of Madhuraj was also the same as Kushalraj. The rulers of both the kingdoms were the descendants of both ministers. They were stone hearted just like their forebears. They showed no leniency towards their subjects. Children were excited when they were leaving for the visit of both kingdoms, but when they were returning to the Glass Palace, their hearts were dampened. A sense of concern for their subjects began to fill their hearts. Mr. Mitral and Miss Sarati sensed this change and viewed it as a positive development. They exchanged smiles, acknowledging the shift.

"Alright! You all head to the Glass Palace. I'll be back in no time!" Mr. Mitral exclaimed.

"Where are you going?" Aravir asked.

Mr. Mitral grinned and replied, "To make things easy for you all."

"What do you mean?"

He was puzzled. Miss Sarati was the only one who grasped the implication behind his words. So, she interjected, "Let him go, everyone! He'll return on his own. Let's move!" They all concurred and departed.

On the other hand, Sriha, Sarath, Aravir, and Ashmi's classmates were engaged in various activities at the Glass Palace. A fellow student brought up a novel game named 'Killer'. Since the game was unfamiliar, he took the initiative to teach it to the group. At that time, Sriha Sarath, Ashmi and Aravir arrived in the Glass Palace along with Miss Sarati. They also heard about the game. When one of their peers was explaining the game, they paused to listen at the entrance.

"In this game, we will make as many chits as there are players. Cop will be written on one chit, and killer will be written on the other. And pawns will be written on the remaining chits. Participants will sit in a circle. After thoroughly mixing the tickets, we'll place them in the center of the circle. Subsequently, each player will pick a chit randomly. The cop's task is to identify the killer."

As that student was describing the game's rules to his peers, Risha (The running gossip queen) interrupted.

"Oh! We're all familiar with this game. We've been playing it since we were kids. What's different about it now?"

The boy responded while showing his palm to her, "I'm not done yet. Please, don't bother me!" Following this, he shifted his attention to his other fellow students and went on to say,

"The killer won't reveal his true identity publicly. Only a cop will disclose his identity in front of everyone. The killer, while evading himself from the gaze of the cop, will signal to the pawns that he is a killer. If a pawn recognizes the killer, he will shout 'I'm dead!' and drop his chit at the center of the circle. This would mean that the killer killed the pawn. And this is how the number of pawns will decrease. Meanwhile, a cop will continue to try to find the killer. If the cop finds out the killer before all the pawns are eliminated, he will win the game. Conversely if the cop fails to find the killer before all the pawns die, the killer will be the winner."

"Interesting!" exclaimed a teacher.

"So, let's play!"

"Yes!" All the students were excited to play the game called 'Killer'.

Every student had gathered in a circle. At the same time, Risha noticed Sriha, Sarath, Ashmi, and Aravir standing at the entrance. She was unable to contain her curiosity, she asked,

"Hey Ashmi, where were you guys? I haven't seen you all since the morning."

As they were aware about her tendency to meddle in other's affairs, Ashmi was on the verge of retaliating, but was interrupted by Miss Sarati, who grabbed her hand.

"They were with me. I had taken them outside to bring some activity props which I had forgotten to carry. I needed four students. So, I asked them to help me out." Miss Sarati clarified.

Risha glanced down towards their holding hands. When Miss Sarati and Ashmi realised it, they immediately left each other's hand.

"Well, where are the props then?" Risha asked, her tone laced with suspicion.

Sarath was positioned behind Miss Sarati, slightly leaning in closer to her as he whispered, "We don't have any props. What will happen now? We're going to get caught, that's for sure!"

Miss Sarati's face remained unchanged, showing no fear. She spoke with confidence. "Mr. Mitral, please bring the props inside."

Mr. Mitral made his way into the Glass Palace, accompanied by four men who were entering the palace one by one, each carrying different items. One man had props for dancing, another man was holding some pastries and sweets, the third man was carrying a camera along with other gear, and the fourth man had musical instruments.

Sriha, Sarath, Ashmi, and Aravir were clueless about what was happening. They believed Miss Sarati was lying to them to protect us, but she wasn't. They looked at Mr. Mitral. He also looked at them and blinked his eyes. At that moment they understood Mr. Mitral had arranged all these things. That's why he had said that he would come later.

"You already had four men working for you, so why did you need four more? Risha asked.

"I wanted to conserve my precious time, therefore, I sent these four students to a different place to gather all these things, so that we could return to the Glass Palace as quickly as possible. These men are only delivering dancing props and other things. They couldn't help us to bring what we wanted. Is there any question left, Risha?" Miss Sarati asked.

"Why just these four? You could've taken other students with you."

"Oh God! She is so annoying! I wish I could throw her out!" Sriha was seething with anger, muttering under her breath.

"Calm down Sriha!" Said Aravir.

Miss Sarati crossed her arms and stated, "If you have forgotten, let me remind you that these four are the heads of the college."

Risha could sense that her constant questioning was making everyone annoyed, so she zipped her mouth then.

"Why do people like this exist in the world? I hate her! I wish she hadn't come on this trip. The environment would have been peaceful without her." Sriha was still fuming.

"It's okay, Sriha! If there were no bad or evil in the world, then no one would appreciate goodness. Therefore, today, we honor King Ashan and King Harishan for their virtuous actions and compassion, while we condemn ministers for their wrongdoings and harshness. Negative people might glow now, but their temporary glow fades quickly. Ultimately, it's good people who truly shine, and their light is eternal! Always keep that in mind. Now, go and enjoy some playtime. Otherwise, they'll doubt us more." Miss Sarati said, and Sriha agreed.

Her words soothed Sriha's frustration. She reflected, "Miss Sarati is correct! We must not let someone else's negative actions affect us." Taking a deep breath, she decided to join Ashmi, Sarath, and Aravir in playing the game 'Killer'.

Later on, while engrossed in their games, they lost track of time and didn't notice the night had fallen. Every student and teacher had their evening meal and retired to their rooms for rest, except for Miss Sarati, Sriha, Ashmi, Sarath, and Aravir.

"So, what's the plan now? What will we do ahead? How do we reclaim our kingdom?" Aravir asked.

"Once this trip ends, head back to your homes and discuss with your parents. We can't fight with them alone. We need the support of many people." Miss Sarati answered.

They all concurred with her advice, because they knew that it could be difficult to fight with them. Their adversaries were well-equipped with numerous weapons, capable of eliminating them swiftly. Thus, they needed to devise a robust plan to overcome them.

SIX

THE REUNION

Srishtika was perched on a chair in her backyard, engrossed in a book, when Sriha arrived with her bag. Upon seeing her, Srishtika rose to greet her.

"How was your journey?" She asked.

"It was pleasant, but..." She paused, unsure of how to respond.

She mulled over it for a moment before suddenly turning her gaze towards her mother, clasping her mother's hands together, and exclaimed,

"Mom, I want to reclaim our kingdom and the Glass Palace!"

Her mother was taken aback by her words and kept looking at her. She was still puzzled by her daughter's declaration, so she was trying to grasp what her daughter said.

"We visited the kingdom of King Ashan and King Harishan during this trip. Miss Sarati and Mr. Mitral had taken us to the kingdoms. And our trip was to the Glass Palace."

Srishtika was shocked. "What! All of you had gone to the Glass Palace. Why? What if something had gone wrong with

"

you all?"

"Don't worry mom, Miss Sarati and Mr. Mitral were with us. How could anything bad happen to us?"

"How did they even know about the Glass Palace and the Kingdoms of King Ashan and King Harishan? Who is Miss Sarati?" She narrowed her eyes and asked in suspicion.

"She is our teacher." She paused, her voice faltering slightly as she continued, "Mom, she was…she was the stewardess of Queen Vedarsha."

When Srishtika heard those words, she got dumbstruck. Then Mr. Mitral came into her mind. She didn't even waste a single second and immediately asked Sriha.

"Who exactly is Mr. Mitral?"

"He claimed to be a resident of King Ashan's realm. King Ashan once assisted him, so now he intends to help us reclaim our heritage. We have also encountered him in our dreams." She answered.

"A resident of King Ashan's realm? How peculiar! Why would anyone aid us for such a minor reason?" She contemplated.

"I wish to meet him."

"Sure! I have no objections. I will set up a meeting for you."

"Great, now you should go and refresh yourself." Srishtika suggested. Sriha nodded and left.

"If Miss Sarati was a stewardess to Queen Vedarsha, then Mr. Mitral cannot be an ordinary person. He must be of royal descent. I need to find out the truth," Srishtika mused.

Later, Anishiv returned home from work. He went straight to Srishtika and stated,

"On my way home, I realized that our children are aware of the entire history of the Glass Palace. They could take any action to reclaim their kingdom. Therefore, we need to act before they make a move."

"They have already begun." Srishtika answered.

"What do you mean?"

"I mean someone else is already guiding them."

"Who is guiding them?" Anishiv asked.

"The stewardess of Queen Vedarsha."

Anishiv was surprised. He was unaware that the stewardess of Queen Vedarsha was still alive. He had not expected that to happen.

"And Mr. Mitral is also guiding them. However, the odd thing is that he isn't disclosing his true identity."

"Do you know his true identity?"

"No, but my instinct says that he must be someone important. He must be a royal person, who knows everything about our lives. Sriha mentioned that they have encountered Mr. Mitral in their dreams as well.

"So, we must meet him."

"Yes! I'm going to meet him tomorrow."

"I will accompany you. Aparvi and Parthan will also come along." Said Anishiv.

Srishtika nodded and updated Parthan and Aparvi about the situation. The next morning, Srishtika, Anishiv, Aparvi, and Parthan got ready to meet Mr. Mitral and Miss Sarati. They were unsure of Mr. Mitral's whereabouts but felt confident that Miss Sarati would possess all the information they required, and she would definitely assist them. Sriha had already informed Miss Sarati that their parents were eager to meet her and Mr. Mitral. Miss Sarati instructed them to gather at the Glass Palace. So, Sriha, Sarath, Ashmi, and Aravir, along with their parents, made their way to the Glass Palace.

When they reached there, they stepped inside the Palace. They noticed that Miss Sarati was already there, standing at a short distance from the throne and gazing intently at it. A whirlwind of emotions swirled within her. While she was lost in her thoughts, Srishtika called out her name loudly so that she could hear them from afar.

"Kasita!"

Kasita was the true name of Miss Sarati. When Srishtika called out to her, she was not surprised as she was already aware of their connection. Kasita turned gently and looked at them with compassionate eyes. Because they were all like her own children. She had devoted her entire life to Queen Vedarsha and her lineage. Srishtika and Aparvi were standing together. Kasita approached them, bowing respectfully.

"Your highness! How are you? I have been waiting for you all."

Then she turned to Anishiv and Parthan, bowing once more, she said,

"Your Majesty, where have you all been?"

When they saw her bowing to each of them, Anishiv halted her with a gentle command.

"Please, do not bow before us, Kasita. We are not King and Queen. You are like a mother to us."

As the four young ones observed this interaction, they felt a shiver run down their spines. The titles of Your Highness and Your Majesty created an entirely different atmosphere for them.

"This is your generosity, Majesty! But now this throne belongs to you all. Following the passing of both the Kings and Queens, you and Parthan shall take on the roles of the new kings, and Srishtika and Aparvi will be the new Queens."

"But we are not worthy of being Kings. We failed to confront our foes. We neglected our responsibilities. We could not protect our legacy. Every time this thought crosses my mind, I feel a deep sense of shame," Parthan expressed.

"It wasn't your fault! That time was not good. Everything arrives at its appropriate moment. Thus, this throne has remained vacant for so many years." Answered Kasita.

"But who will perform the coronation? I wish there was someone from the royal lineage still alive." Said Aparvi.

"Who says that no one is alive?"

When Kasita said this, the four of them exchanged puzzled glances with her. Kasita perceived their confusion. She beamed and said,

"Allow me to introduce you all to someone."

Kasita glanced towards the main entrance door. Others around her also turned to look. They saw an elderly man making his way into the Glass Palace. As his face came into view, Srishtika, Aparvi, Parthan, and Anishiv were taken aback.

"Mom, that's Mr. Mitral," Aravir exclaimed.

Aparvi was too stunned to catch Aravir's words; she was still reeling from the sight of him in the Glass Palace.

"Grandsire!" she gasped in astonishment.

Upon hearing that term, Aravir murmured in confusion, "Grandsire?"

Aparvi moved closer to Grandsire, feeling a surge of emotions both joy and nostalgia upon seeing him alive after so many years. Grandsire, equally delighted, greeted her warmly. She rushed to him and touched his feet in reverence.

"How are you, Aparvi?" Grandsire asked gently, compassionately placing his hand on Aparvi's head.

"I'm good, Grandsire! What about you? I thought you might have died when the minister attacked us." Said Aparvi.

"I was out of town that day. But when I returned to the kingdom, I was devastated to witness such a painful scenario." Grandsire replied, his eyes welling with tears.

When Anishiv saw him like this, he decided to lighten the mood. He said,

"Grandsire! I'm here too!"

Grandsire turned to him and responded, "I know! How could I ever forget you, Anishiv?" He chuckled lightly.

Seeing the two of them together brought smiles to everyone else's faces. Anishiv embraced Grandsire, and then he bent down to touch his feet. Parthan and Srishtika also approached to seek his blessings. Later, they all noticed the puzzled expressions on Sriha, Sarath, Ashmi, and Aravir's faces. Aparvi stepped forward and said,

"He is my Grandsire."

"And mine too! You always overlook me," Anishiv chimed in.

"That's right! Children, Aparvi is my granddaughter, and Anishiv is also my grandson," Grandsire said with a laugh, playfully teasing him.

"Huh! You also enjoy teasing me, Grandsire!" Anishiv said while getting annoyed.

"But you mentioned that you were merely a resident of King Ashan's realm. How can you then be our Grandsire?" Ashmi asked.

"I had to lie! At that moment, everything was unfamiliar to all of you. You wouldn't have been able to comprehend it. Hence, I believed it could be the best to disclose the truth step by step. If I had revealed everything at once, it would have been difficult to grasp the truth." He explained.

"You're right!" Said Ashmi.

After sharing some delightful moments of their reunion, they decided to take a tour of the Glass Palace.

"Ah! It feels like ages since I last saw the Glass Palace. I missed it terribly," Srishtika expressed as they wandered through the palace. They were all engrossed in old memories.

"We are descendants of King Ashan and King Harishan. How could we possibly neglect our responsibilities? How could we forget our Glass Palace and our kingdom?" Parthan lamented, filled with remorse.

Others were also paying attention to him. They too felt remorseful and guilty for failing to fulfill their responsibilities. They had realized their mistake. Grandsire noticed their distressed expressions. He felt joy that his family had reunited and understood their mistake.

"Let the past remain in the past! We cannot alter what has already taken place. Perhaps it was simply meant to be. And no one can change what fate has inscribed. Now we must concentrate on creating a brighter future." Grandsire expressed.

Due to Grandsire's words, a flicker of hope and bravery ignited within them. Albeit they were uncertain about their next steps. Therefore, Aparvi asked,

"So, what's our plan? How are we going to reclaim our properties?"

"We must confront them. This is the only option. Because they are not going to give our properties to us at all." Sarath said.

"No, we can't fight with them alone. We have to build a huge army." Answered Grandsire.

"How will we manage that? We have nothing right now." Srishtika said anxiously.

"It is possible!" Grandsire exclaimed with a smile. "Kings have treaties with the rulers of many states. I still remember one of my friends, who had promised me that he would stand by me through all my highs and lows."

"Who was that friend?" Anishiv asked.

"He is my closest friend, King Suhadh! The bond we share is as profound as the connection between King Ashan and King Harishan. It's hard to express, but friendship runs in our veins," he chuckled.

"Then why didn't King Suhadh come to rescue our families?" Parthan questioned.

"That was an unexpected attack. King Suhadh was unaware of it! But if I ask him for his help today, I am certain he would promptly prepare to aid us," Grandsire asserted confidently.

"Isn't he aware that you are alive? Didn't he receive the news about that sudden attack on the Glass Palace?" Srishtika asked.

"Did you know that I was alive?" Grandsire posed.

Srishtika grasped the implication of Grandsire's question and shook her head, indicating no.

"When you all see us together, all your doubts will vanish in a moment. We must travel to King Suhadh's realm to seek his help. He will undoubtedly help us. No one can stand before his huge army. He holds immense power!" Said Grandsire.

They all concurred with Grandsire. Srishtika, Anishiv, Parthan, and Aparvi had reunited with Grandsire after many years. Grandsire had also met his great-grandchildren for the first time. The hearts of each one of them brimmed with joy and affection. For years, they had longed for these cherished moments. Consequently, they were so engaged that they hardly noticed how the entire day slipped away.

Sriha, Aravir, Ashmi, and Sarath huddled around their Grandsire, listening intently as he recounted the history of their kingdom and lineage. They were captivated by his stories. Amidst the serious discussions, Grandsire shared some humorous anecdotes too, and their laughter resonated throughout the Glass Palace. In the midst of this all, no one realized when they all drifted off to sleep right there.

The following morning, they all prepared to visit the kingdom of Grandsire's friend, King Suhadh.

"Until we reclaim our kingdom and the Glass Palace, we will not return home," Srishtika announced to everyone.

"Yes! We are now determined to claim what belongs to us, no matter what," declared Anishiv.

"Alright then, let us make a vow to fight for our rights until our last breath." Grandsire said, extending his hand towards them. They all joined him, placing their hands over Grandsire's hand.

"We pledge to battle for our heritage and preserve our legacy. We will fight until our last breath," they proclaimed together with determination.

Due to this declaration, a wave of uplifting energy stirred within their hearts. A sense of assurance blossomed inside them, leading them to believe that victory was now certain. There is a saying, 'What you think, you become.' They projected a positive energy into the universe, and in turn, the cosmos echoed back, instilling in them a sense of victory. This is how the law of attraction works. 'What you feel, manifests.'

Soon after, they were prepared to embark on their journey to the realm of King Suhadh. As they exited the Glass Palace, they were greeted by a stunning atmosphere with a refreshing breeze blowing. This gentle wind reminded Sriha of her dream, where she found herself trapped in a terrifying whirlwind.

"Hold on!"

Upon hearing her call, everyone stopped. Srishtika asked,

"What's the matter, Sriha?"

"I forgot to ask you something. We had an unusual dream earlier."

Grandsire stepped forward and asked, "What was the dream about?"

"I was in a beautiful location when suddenly a chilly breeze morphed into a menacing tornado. The fascinating part was that I could control the tornado. What could this signify?"

As Sarath, Ashmi, and Aravir listened to her talking about the tornado, they too stepped forward to share their own dreams. Grandsire understood the situation and looked at their parents' astonished expressions. He discreetly signaled them with a blink before shifting his focus back to the children. He said,

"Sriha, I also forgot to mention one more important thing to you all. You were able to tame the whirlwind because you possess the power of the air."

The moment he uttered those words; Sriha was taken aback. Grandsire then elaborated,

"Aravir wields the power of water, Ashmi possesses the ability to destroy anything, and Sarath has the power of fire. Each of you is endowed with unique powers. This is common in our lineage. Every generation inherits these extraordinary abilities from their ancestors."

"It means our parents have those powers too." Sriha guessed.

Grandsire confirmed with a nod. Sarath then turned to Srishtika and asked, "Was this the reason you never allowed us to get close to these things?"

Srishtika nodded. "I wanted to keep you all unaware of these powers, as revealing them could expose the truth of the Glass Palace and it could have been dangerous."

"How can we use these powers?" Aravir asked.

"We will teach you later. But right now, we must leave." Grandsire replied.

Afterwards, Grandsire along with his family reached the kingdom of King Suhadh. The gatekeeper of the palace relayed the message to King Suhadh.

"Oh king, few people have come to meet you. One of them claims to be your dearest friend."

"My dearest friend! Who might that person be?" King Suhadh wondered. "Bring them in." He commanded his gatekeeper.

After a few moments, Grandsire came to the assembly along with his family and stood before the king who was seated on his throne. Grandsire's eyes were sparkling because of tears, and a broad smile graced his face. King Suhadh noticed that, and he asked,

"Who are you? And why are you in tears? I heard you consider yourself as my closest friend!"

"Perhaps you have forgotten me," Grandsire replied.

King Suhadh appeared puzzled. He kept observing him for a while, trying to recognize him. Suddenly, a memory struck him, and a broad grin spread across his face.

"Vasud! My old friend!" He jumped up from his throne and approached Grandsire.

"How have you been, my friend?" he exclaimed as he wrapped his arms around him. Both were filled with ecstasy.

After, clasping his hands together, he said, "I truly apologize, Vasud! I failed to recognize you. I'm aging, and my memory is fading with each passing day. Please forgive me." Tears welled up in his eyes.

"There's no need to apologize, Suhadh! It's not your fault. We are meeting after so many years, so it's understandable!" Grandsire reassured him as he gently lowered King Suhadh's joined hands.

The families of Grandsire and King Suhadh were delighted to witness their joyful reunion. It stirred emotions in the hearts of all present. Later on, King Suhadh extended a welcome to them in the finest way possible. Once they were settled in the King's chamber, the king said,

"Vasud, I had no idea that you were still alive. When I learned about that heart-wrenching war, I rushed to your Glass Palace, but I saw that no one was alive there. All I could see were lifeless bodies strewn across the palace grounds. All I could see were lifeless bodies strewn across the palace grounds. Among them were the remains of King Ashan, King Harishan, Queen Vedarsha, and the soldiers. Some of the corpses were beyond recognition. I did not find your body, nor that of Queen Kauriya or their children. I was uncertain about your demise. Therefore, I sent my soldiers to search for all of you. Unfortunately, they returned empty-handed. Ultimately, I lost hope and assumed that you all had died as well."

"I anticipated that you would look for us," Grandsire replied.

"But where have you been all these years?" King Suhadh inquired.

"I was not in the Glass Palace during the battle. When I returned to the palace, I came to know that the ministers had attacked and killed my entire family. I hurried to find them, but I was too late. Just like you, I also witnessed the dead bodies scattered throughout the palace. It was a heart throbbing sight that was hard to accept. I was at a loss for what to do. Then, as I glanced out of the window, I spotted someone lying by the lake's edge. Upon closer inspection, I recognized her. It was none other than Queen Kauriya. I rushed to the lakeshore and gently cradled her head in my lap, trying to revive her."

Flashback...,

"Kauriya! Are you alright? What happened? Where are my grandchildren?" Grandsire asked with concern.

Queen Kauriya was taking her few last breaths. She mustered all her strength to speak to the Grandsire. She said,

"I...I had ordered my...my children to flee from...from the palace. They are safe!" She was stammering while talking to him.

Afterward, she grasped Grandsire's hand and urged, "Grand...Grandsire, swear to me that you will save our heritage. I want you to refrain from seeking assistance from anyone to reclaim our kingdom until my children develop a firm determination in their hearts. If...if the desire to regain their kingdom stirs within them, they will fight to get what belongs to them and will also value and appreciate the hard-earned kingdom. I...I need you to instill in them the values and discipline required. Teach them the responsibilities of a king and queen and how they ought to conduct themselves. At a very young age, they have lost their parents. I am entrusting their future to you. Now, it is in your hands to shape it. Please promise me! I don't have much time left." She said, reaching her trembling hand toward Grandsire.

Grandsire didn't hesitate for a moment before placing his hand over Queen Kauriya's hand.

"I promise!" As Grandsire gave his word, Queen Kauriya took her last breath.

A tear rolled down Grandsire's cheek. He had lost everything in a single day.

The flashback concludes.

Everyone's eyes were glistening with tears. No one could find the words to say. The palace was enveloped in silence, as if everyone was grieving a loss.

"I was alone at that time, and it was nearly impossible for me to carry out the last rites for all those who had passed away there. So, I went to ask for help for the cremations. However, when I returned with a few men, I discovered that no one was there. I then thought that perhaps someone else might have performed their last rites, but still I wanted to confirm, therefore, I made my way to the crematorium and found that everyone had been cremated. I scanned the area but couldn't locate anyone. It's possible that the person who accomplished this had left before I arrived." He inhaled deeply and continued, "I am truly thankful to that person. I simply wish to meet him once and express my gratitude. But I have no idea if that kind soul is still alive."

Viharsh, the minister of King Suhadh, smiled gently and responded, "Grandsire, that person is indeed alive, and he is none other than your beloved friend, King Suhadh."

When the Grandsire heard that, he immediately looked towards King Suhadh.

"Was that person you?" He asked in astonishment.

King Suhadh nodded in affirmation. The Grandsire's eyes brimmed with tears. He went near him and knelt down before him, bringing both his hands together as he spoke,

"How can I thank you, my friend? I was at the verge of despair at that time. Overwhelmed by the sorrow of losing my dear ones, I was unable to act. I was in a fragile state. Yet, as always, you arrived just like a divine being and took charge of everything. I am at a loss as to how I might repay you, my friend." He broke down as he spoke.

King Suhadh rushed to him and helped him to his feet. With a kind heart, he said,

"It was not a favor, Vasud! It was my responsibility. There's a saying, 'A friend in need is a friend indeed!' Why do you see my actions as a favor? If the roles were reversed, and you were in my position, wouldn't you have offered your help?"

"Of course, I would have come to help you!"

"Exactly! It was my responsibility as a friend. The struggles in your life cause me twice the heartache. Always keep that in mind!" Said King Suhadh.

The Grandsire nodded, and they embraced each other. When Srishtika, Anishiv, Aparvi and Parthan witnessed this moment, Srishtika mumbled,

"How genuine their friendship is! I was doubting for no reason."

Anishiv caught her whispering, he smiled, and replied, "Exactly! Did you not hear what Grandsire said?"

"What?"

"Friendship flows in our blood!" Anishiv answered and they both chuckled.

Their children (Aravir, Sriha, Ashmi and Sarath) were also witnessing all those beautiful moments and learning all those things. The Grandsire's promise to Queen Kauriya to instill discipline in her children and shape their future well was almost fulfilled. He was not only influencing the futures of Queen Vedarsha and Queen Kauriya's children but also setting a positive example for his great-grandchildren. While shaping their futures, he was also unwittingly instilling good values in them.

The next morning, the Grandsire decided to explain the reason for their visit to King Suhadh. He entered his chamber and stated,

"Friend, as you are already aware that our entire property is under the control of the Minister's children, Rahu and Saddhant. I want my property back! It is our ancestral land, and I do not want to lose it at any cost. Therefore, we have made a firm decision to reclaim our property, and that is why we are here to seek your help."

"I know! I understand, and even if you had not requested my assistance, I would have undoubtedly lent a hand." King Suhadh replied courteously.

Grandsire smiled at his statement and said, "As you already know how dangerous those people are! I cannot afford to lose my family again. Now, their end is necessary. I will require a vast army to confront them."

King Suhadh smiled gently and said, "Don't worry! The entire force of my empire will be with you. This time, our victory is assured. We will vanquish those fiends at any cost."

Meanwhile, King Rahu's secret operative overheard their conversation and headed to Kushalraj to inform his king.

"King Rahu, I have learned that the Grandsire of Madhuraj is still alive, and he is scheming against us to reclaim his throne."

"Do not refer to it as his kingdom, you fool. It is my kingdom! My father fought for it!" King Rahu erupted at him.

King Rahu was actually the son of Tushyan (the minister of King Ashan). King Rahu was just like his father. In fact, he was even more malevolent than his father Tushyan. After his father's death, he started ruling over Kushalraj and appointed his younger brother Saddhant as the king of Madhuraj.

King Harishan's minister Shangir had already been killed by the king. However, his two sons were alive and also demanded their portion of the kingdom and the Glass Palace.

"King Rahu, our fathers agreed to distribute all the wealth equally," stated minister Shangir's son.

Since King Rahu was also evil like his father Tushyan, he grinned maliciously and replied,

"Of course, you will get your share! Commander, bring their share." King Rahu commanded his officer to comply.

King Rahu's commander came and stood in front of Shangir's sons, hiding something behind his back. Shangir's sons were elated to know that King Rahu was giving them their share in the kingdoms. However, King Rahu's malevolent intentions had planned something else. the commander swiftly drew his sword and plunged it into their stomachs. As they collapsed, one son perished immediately, while the other, gasping for breath. While writhing in pain he said,

"Oh King Rahu! You have deceived me. I place a curse upon you; what could never belong to me shall not belong to you either." With that curse, he passed away.

King Rahu was filled with pride. He declared his disbelief in such matters and erupted into loud laughter.

Afterwards, King Rahu also attempted to enter the Glass Palace, unaware of the curse placed by King Ashan. Fortunately, one of the soldiers went first towards the Glass

Palace before King Rahu. As the soldier got closer, the brightness of the glass walls intensified, and he could not withstand the dazzling rays; it felt as though he was engulfed in flames. He thought it was merely the sun's rays affecting him, so he ignored the sensation and hurried to open the palace door, hoping to find relief inside. However, the moment he touched the door, the brightness surged even more, searing his entire body, leading to his immediate death from excruciating pain.

King Rahu was taken aback and horrified by this heart-rending scene. He was confused about how this could have occurred, so he tried to approach the palace, but soon felt the same burning sensation throughout his body, therefore he immediately retreated. He could not muster the courage to go close to the Glass Palace again and went back to his kingdom.

The Glass Palace was an enchanted structure. It was impossible to own the palace, Therefore, King Rahu resolved to find something that could break the spell of the Glass Palace. Yet, all his endeavors proved fruitless.

On the other hand, Kasita was standing on the balcony, her face etched with worry. Grandsire noticed her lost in thoughts and went to her, he asked,

"Kasita, is there something that is bothering you?"

"When King Ashan had cursed the ministers, he had declared that only his heirs would be able to enter into the palace, and that is precisely what transpired."

"So, isn't that a good thing? King Rahu couldn't enter the palace. What's wrong with it? Why do you seem so anxious?"

"I'm concerned because the curse has been eliminated from the Glass palace. The Glass Palace is no longer bound by any kind of enchantment since the descendants of the

Glass Palace have arrived. Now, if someone attempts to step inside, they won't face any danger. I fear what might occur if King Rahu finds out about this. He will undoubtedly attempt to take control of the Glass Palace."

"Don't fret, Kasita! There is no need to worry. If this hadn't happened, we wouldn't be here today. It was an essential step." Grandsire said.

Grandsire called his great grandchildren, Sriha, Sarath, Aravir and Ashmi and told them to sit with him. The four promptly complied with Grandsire's request.

"We are soon going to wage a war against Rahu and Saddhant. They are both ruthless sons of minister Tushyan. Therefore, it's important for all of you to be prepared. While none of you are trained warriors, you are fortunate to have distinct abilities that can help you protect yourselves and others. Nevertheless, you must work diligently to master the skills required to wield your superpowers. If you don't put in the necessary effort, those powers will not be of any use. Today, I will teach you how to activate your superpowers. Whenever you wish to use your abilities, you must concentrate on that specific skill and your goal. When you think about it with pure intent, you'll be able to tap into your powers. Now, let's give it a try!"

Grandsire had already set up some equipment for them. He first called Sriha to come forward and try her superpower. She had the power to manipulate and generate wind.

"You have to blow that piece of wood hanging from the tree. After focusing on your abilities and your target, when you stretch out your hand with an open palm towards the wood, it will blow away," Grandsire instructed.

Sriha thought about her power and aimed her target, then she stretched out her hand, but the dangling wood didn't budge even a little.

"Sriha, you are still not properly concentrating in your mind. Don't regard the hanging wood as just an ordinary object," Grandsire remarked.

She attempted several more times, but nothing occurred. She let out a sigh in disappointment. She was struggling to harness her powers. Grandsire thought to himself,

'This isn't going to work like this; I need to find another way to awaken her abilities.'

Grandsire picked up another sturdy piece of wood and suddenly hurled it towards Sriha. Everyone gasped. Sriha was also alarmed, causing her body to instinctively react. In a bid to protect herself, she extended her hand with an open palm towards the wood. As she did so, a powerful gust of wind erupted from her palm, sending the wood tumbling away. Everyone was left speechless by the sight.

Grandsire beamed with satisfaction. Sriha was taken aback. She inquired, "How did that happen?"

"When I threw the wood at you, it frightened you. You wanted to defend yourself, so your mind focused on the wood. Your mind captured that emotion and zeroed in on the target. That's how it works! You need to concentrate on your target and aim for it without allowing other thoughts to intrude."

Then he called Aravir, who possessed the ability to control water. At first, he was also unable to harness his power. However, after focusing and practicing for a bit longer, he achieved success. He could conjure tornadoes within the water and even calm it when the waves became turbulent. Sarath had the fire element within him. The flames had the potential to incinerate anyone, which was already daunting for him. When Grandsire instructed him to douse the flames of the campfire, Sarath's mind was already focused on not getting hurt. And as he waved his hand over the flames, it was extinguished.

Next came Ashmi's turn; Ashmi had the ability to shatter anything. When Grandsire was tossing objects at her, she was instinctively trying to evade them. Grandsire knew that she wouldn't be able to break the stones in one go, therefore he was throwing lighter items her way to prevent any harm. He advised her,

"Stop trying to evade by moving aside repeatedly; you need to confront the obstacles in front of you. Stand firm and combat them."

The fear of getting hurt still lingered within her. Grandsire thought that now he would have to hurl a large, heavy stone at her. Only this could help her overcome her fear. He thought if things spiraled out of control, he would intervene and save her. He then lifted a hefty stone and threw it toward her. She was about to run away from there, but paused and thought to herself,

'How many times will you run away, Ashmi? You must face this and fight it.'

Then she summoned up the courage, just as she had done in her dreams, she made a fist as the stone came closer to her and abruptly thrust her hand forward. When her fist struck the stone, it scattered into pieces.

Grandsire, Sriha, Sarath and Aravir were curious to see what would happen. When she broke the stone, they burst into applause.

"Yes, we did it!" Aravir exclaimed with joy.

"But it's not enough, each of you must continue to practice until you fully master this skill. If you stop practicing, you will lose your art. To keep your art alive, consistent practice is essential. That's all for today." Grandsire instructed.

Every day, the four of them trained rigorously to attain mastery over their superpowers. Grandsire also showed them how to wield different weapons. Because Grandsire knew that they would encounter numerous challenges during the war and would need to defend themselves. This is why he was providing them with thorough training. Their parents were already familiar with all these weapons, yet they persisted in practicing since they hadn't utilized them in quite a while. They also possessed the same abilities as their offspring. Two years went by, and they were steadily honing their skills and gearing up for battle.

One day, a commander of King Rahu rushed to him, panting heavily. Upon noticing him, King Rahu inquired,

"What happened, commander? Have you brought any bad news?"

The commander replied, "No, King! I have brought good news. You had asked me to discover a way to lift the curse from the Glass Palace, and I have been searching for a solution. Today, I discovered that two years ago, some individuals entered the Glass Palace with a group of children. Remarkably, nothing befell them. They were wandering around the palace with ease. It seems the power of the Glass Palace may be waning or possibly has vanished."

King Rahu was taken aback upon hearing this news. He quickly made his way to the Glass Palace. When he reached there, he went near the palace cautiously. Remembering his previous encounter, he was scared and hesitated, then he extended his hand slowly towards the door of the Glass Palace. When his hand was just an inch apart, he shut his eyes tightly and abruptly pushed the door and then swiftly retracted his hand. When he felt no pain or burning sensation, he gradually opened his eyes. To his relief, nothing had harmed him, and the door had swung open. He was on cloud nine due to extreme happiness, lifting his spirit immensely. He erupted into loud laughter, as if he had achieved a monumental victory. Stepping into the Glass Palace, he took the first few moments admiring the palace. He strolled throughout the entire palace. Eventually, when he returned to the grand courtroom, he spotted a throne studded with crystals. Overcome with excitement, he couldn't resist and promptly took a seat on the splendid throne. However, as soon as he settled down, he crashed to the floor with a loud thud. He struggled to remain seated, but each attempt ended with him tumbling down again. The joy that had filled him moments before evaporated, replaced by anger. In a fit of rage, he struck his fist against the throne. As soon as he banged his fist on the throne, a voice echoed,

"You cannot be entitled to this throne. This throne can only be attained through loyalty and diligence."

King Rahu began to scan his surroundings to find the source of the voice. However, he was unable to spot anyone.

He was initially furious for a few seconds, but soon he calmed down and thought, 'Even if I can't sit on the throne of the Glass Palace, the fact that I can enter it means that it now belongs to me. I've been waiting for this moment for years. I knew that Grandsire would surely come and break the curse to enter the Glass Palace, therefore, I didn't attack Grandsire even after he was alive. But now, I must eliminate Grandsire to finish his entire lineage; otherwise, that old man will attempt to seize my Glass Palace once again. This time, I will make sure that no one from Grandsire's family survives.' He laughed.

He quickly made his way back to Kushalraj and, after scribbling a message on a letter, instructed his commander to deliver it to the kingdom of King Suhadh.

Later, a messenger of King Suhadh arrived and presented a letter to him. King Suhadh opened the letter. The letter was like:

"Dear Grandsire,

As you always say, only wicked and cowardly people strike from behind; those who possess strength confront their foes openly. Thus, I declare war. We both want the throne, we both desire power, leaving us with no alternative but the war! Whoever will win, will get the throne of both kingdoms and the Glass Palace.

Your adversary, King Rahu."

After reading the letter, King Suhadh hurried to Grandsire without wasting a moment.

"Vasudh!" He called out his name loudly as he went towards him.

Grandsire heard his voice and turned to face him. Noticing the anxiety etched on his face, he asked,

"What happened, Suhadh? Why do you seem so distressed?"

"Rahu knows you are alive, and he has also sent a message for you." he responded, handing the letter to Grandsire.

Grandsire perused the letter and said, "The moment we have been waiting for has finally arrived."

War, just the mention of it can evoke a sense of dread, war that obliterates everything, war that concludes victory or defeat. But these physical wars are much smaller than the wars within us. When a man cannot conquer the turmoil within, that inner strife often takes the form of a huge war outside.

A few days later, as Grandsire was preparing for an impending battle, he summoned Sriha, Aparvi, Kasita,

Srishtika, and Ashmi. He stated, "Pay close attention to what I say; during the battle, King Rahu will surely try to make his way to the Glass Palace as soon as he gets a chance. He is the kind of person who cannot bear to see others relish what he cannot obtain for himself. Therefore, he will likely attempt to bring harm to the Glass Palace. So, during the battle, you all have to protect the Glass Palace and its throne. My instincts tell me that King Rahu will make an effort to damage the throne, because he cannot see anyone else becoming the owner of the Glass Palace."

They all agreed with him. However, there was another man nearby, discreetly eavesdropping on their discussion. He was none other than a secret operative of King Rahu. He had been monitoring them ever since King Rahu learned about Grandsire being alive. The secret agent swiftly made his way to Kushalraj, but enroute to the kingdom, he overheard some subjects from King Suhadh's realm discussing the Glass Palace. Consequently, he paused to listen in on their exchange.

One of the people said, "Have you heard? Grandsire Vasud has returned after so many years to safeguard his Glass Palace. I think the throne of the Glass Palace holds immense power, which is why people are still fighting for it even after so many years."

"Yes, I think so too! As we can see, Grandsire and his entire clan possess great strength. The foes killed King Harishan and King Ashan merely to seize the throne of the Glass Palace. Perhaps the real power lies within that throne," another person responded.

"You are right! I have seen that palace from outside. It is magnificent! I wonder how it looks on the inside?"

Upon hearing this, King Rahu's secret agent immediately went to Kushalraj to inform King Rahu everything.

"Oh King, Grandsire is dispatching half of his forces along with some of his loyal people to protect the Glass Palace. He suspects that you might try to invade the Glass Palace and damage both the palace and its throne. Therefore, he is proactively preparing to shield his legacy from any potential threats of the future. Additionally, I overheard some people discussing the throne of the Glass Palace, they were saying that they feel the real power of the Glass Palace lies in its throne." reported the secret agent.

"If the true might of the Glass Palace is indeed in its throne, what would occur if it were to be destroyed?" Questioned King Rahu's commander, a sinister grin spread across his face as he looked at King Rahu.

"Commander, what are you implying?" King Rahu asked.

"If we destroy the throne of the Glass Palace, their strength will automatically diminish."

Both King Rahu and his commander exchanged a devilish smirk.

King Rahu burst into a loud laughter and said, "How foolish they are! They don't even have any clue that we are aware of their entire conspiracy."

While King Rahu and his commander were laughing, his minister fell into his thoughts. When King Rahu noticed this, he asked,

"What's troubling you, minister? Aren't you happy?"

"I have a question. If you destroy the Glass Palace and its throne, how will you become the king of the Glass Palace?"

"I hate to say this, but Grandsire is incredibly clever. He knows precisely how to protect his Glass Palace. He has left no option for anyone to ascend to the throne of the Glass Palace. He has eliminated all the possibilities of me. Therefore, if I cannot become the king, I will ensure that no one else can also take the ownership of the Glass Palace." King Rahu replied with a smirk.

SEVEN

THE WAR

At the dawn of the day, Grandsire, Aravir, Sarath, Anishiv, Parthan, King Suhadh, and his sons were prepared to march to the battlefield alongside a vast army. Whereas, Sriha, Srishtika, Aparvi, Kasita, and Ashmi made their way to the Glass Palace. Shortly before departing for battle, Aravir and Sarath approached Grandsire and bowed to touch his feet to seek his blessings. This gesture profoundly touched Grandsire, who lifted them both to their feet and took them into his embrace.

"I cannot predict how many will return once the war concludes, but my blessings will forever be with each of you. Victory is assured for all of you!" Grandsire proclaimed, holding them tightly once more.

This heartfelt exchange brought tears to the eyes of everyone present. After a few moments, they mounted their chariots, put on their armor, and set off toward the battlefield. Parthan was the commander of his force.

On the battlefield.

They were all positioned in front of one another. One faction embodied malevolence, while the other represented virtue. The malevolent faction sought victory driven by their own greed, whereas the virtuous faction aimed for triumph out of a sense of justice. Every individual on both sides had a fierce determination in their mind and it was clearly visible in their eyes. No one was prepared to accept defeat. An intense battle was impending on the field, but internally, a war had been waged for a long time. Meanwhile, those anxiously awaiting the return of their beloved, who had gone to fight, were fervently praying for their safety and success, as the dread of losing them grew heavier in their hearts. For a moment, silence enveloped the entire battlefield. Each warrior stood poised for the impending conflict. Soon after, the war drums started to beat, and the sound of conches echoed all around, which awoke the enthusiasm in each of the warrior's hearts. The grand war had commenced.

Parthan firmed his grip on his sword and surged toward his adversaries. The foes charged back at them as if they would kill them in a single blow. The entire forces of both factions clashed and pounced upon each other. The battlefield reverberated with the noise of colliding swords, the thud of punches, the cries of combatants, the whizzing of arrows being released, and the agonized shouts resulting from swords piercing the bodies.

Grandsire was aware about the formidable strength of King Rahu, and the unsettling fact was that King Rahu could betray at any moment. He would never engage in battle with integrity. Grandsire was acutely aware of his malicious intentions and nature. Therefore, he decided to confront King Rahu. The soldiers and generals of King Rahu formed a protective barrier around King Rahu as Grandsire and his force moved towards them. Sarath and Aravir launched an attack on the sons of King Rahu. Like their forebears, King Rahu's sons were also wicked. Parthan swung away his chariot to do a combat with the soldiers of King Rahu. Lethiferous arrows from the soldiers left the blows but failed to hit the target as the opponent's arrows destroyed them in midair.

King Rahu had two sons named Madhul and Ravin. Saddhant, the younger brother of King Rahu, also had two sons named Jayan and Kishit.

Madhul directly pounced upon Aravir. Both of their swords were clashing with each other and countering the attack they were getting from each other. When Madhul surrounded Aravir along with his fellow warriors, Aravir contemplated,

'He is hell-bent on killing me. That is why he is targeting me with groups, aiming to wear me down. Now is the time for me to unleash my superpowers.'

With that thought, he dismounted from his chariot and jabbed his sword into the ground and closed his eyes, after a couple of seconds, he opened his eyes and attacked Madhul with his superpowers. Aravir unleashed a torrent of water upon him, which was emanating from his hands. The sheer force of his attack propelled Madhul and his chariot several miles away, leaving him writhing in agony.

On the other hand, Sarath was engaged in a battle with the second son of King Rahu, Ravin. Ravin had also come with many warriors with him. Sarath jumped out of his chariot with mace in his hand. He swirled his mace above his head and started moving ahead. One by one, he was hitting his mace upon each soldier's head coming his way. Witnessing the wrath of Sarath, many soldiers turned tail and fled the battlefield, desperate to save their lives. Ravin, with bloodshot eyes, looked at Sarath. He also leaped out of his chariot and pounced upon Sarath. Ravin was also a formidable warrior, his one powerful strike sent Sarath crashing to the ground. However, the royal blood was flowing in Sarath's veins, Sarath rose once more to confront him and retaliated against his strikes. But that was not enough to kill a demon like Ravin. Therefore, he attacked him with a ball of fire, which was his superpower, a power of fire. Unfortunately, Ravin also had evil power, so he dismissed the fireball midair with his own forceful blow. Sarath's patience was coming to an end, so he showered a barrage of fireballs at Ravin. While Ravin was preoccupied with deflecting these furious attacks, Sarath leapt high into the air and struck his mace crashing down upon Ravin's head. That fatal strike resulted in Ravin's immediate demise.

The elements of water and fire drew the attention of King Rahu. He saw that his two sons had been knocked down by Aravir and Sarath. The grandsire also observed this occurrence. King Rahu was shocked and rushed towards them. Upon seeing their condition, fury surged within him, and his eyes glowed with rage. King Rahu had been unaware that they too possessed such powers.

"They also have these powers!" He mumbled.

The Grandsire went there and laughed at his mumbling. He said, "Rahu, what were you expecting? Did you think they would be like your sons? Have you forgotten, or did your father forget to inform you that it is our royal tradition to pass down our extraordinary powers to our heirs? Even after we bestow our powers to the next generation, we do not relinquish our own."

King Rahu was taken aback and stepped back two paces. The grandsire laughed once more and said, "Poor Rahu! You've lost your game."

After a brief pause, King Rahu regained his composure and said, "Have you also forgotten that I have superpowers too?"

The Grandsire smiled gently and replied, "Of course I am aware of that! But your motives are malevolent, and regardless of your strength, you will ultimately lose the battle because your wickedness will lead to your downfall. Good will always prevail over evil!"

"I refuse to accept defeat. I will avenge my sons' death and win this battle by any means necessary. Just wait and watch, Grandsire Vasud!" Said King Rahu with rage.

He then rushed towards Grandsire and launched a frenzy upon him. However, Grandsire was also a warrior. He managed to save himself from a frenzied attack. Grandsire and King Rahu were locked in a fierce battle. At that moment, King Rahu used his evil superpowers and struck Grandsire with all his might, then Grandsire also countered his blows with his own extraordinary powers. Their magical forces clashed in the air and were obliterated. Both warriors were exerting their full might in their assaults, extending their hands, yet neither was willing to yield. While engaged in combat with King Rahu, Grandsire said,

"Rahu, you should give up! You will never get the Glass Palace. I have returned with my entire clan. Now you cannot defeat us. So, it would be wise for you to surrender!"

King Rahu chuckled and replied, "Have you forgotten, Grandsire, that my father Tushyan vanquished your son, King Harishan?"

"Tushyan was a coward! He attacked from behind. He had betrayed my son, yet King Harishan triumphed in that battle. Your father also died then, he wanted to become the king and revel in the Glass Palace's delights, but he couldn't achieve his ambition."

Upon hearing this, King Rahu's fury intensified, and he put forth all his power to conquer the battle against Grandsire. Grandsire, in turn, summoned all his strength, eager to demonstrate the might of his clan and the force of righteousness. As Grandsire's strike fell heavily on King Rahu, he could not withstand it and crashed to the ground with a thud and started groaning in agony.

On the other hand, a herd of troops came rushing towards Sarath, so he shot a massive fireball at them, annihilating them all in an instant. Similarly, Aravir was battling alone against another faction of soldiers. He, too, unleashed his powers, creating a devastating water tornado that caused the entire group to collapse simultaneously. Their powers were creating a marvelous spectacle on the battlefield, but it was getting dangerous.

The sound of fireballs, whirlwind, clashing swords, thrusting spears, piercing arrows, deadly blows of the maces were heart-wrenching. The most perilous sight, however, was the wrath of the warriors.

Anishiv was engaged in a battle with Saddhant. Saddhant was equally formidable and had taken down numerous soldiers in a single strike, but Anishiv was no less fierce. He was adamant and putting up a valiant fight as well. It was difficult to defeat him. Saddhant began unleashing a barrage of arrows at Anishiv. The rapidity with which he fired the arrows was so intense for Anishiv that he had to struggle to shield himself from the arrows and retaliate. In response, Anishiv shot a couple of arrows at Saddhant's chariot and shattered it. Saddhant tumbled down. Following that, Anishiv instructed his charioteer to maneuver his chariot around Saddhant. He then attacked with his sword, which caused several scratches on Saddhant's body. Saddhant let out a furious roar and grabbed Anishiv's sword with force. That sudden pull made Anishiv fall too. Subsequently, they engaged in one-on-one combat. Saddhant was dominating, however Anishiv was also not giving up. The war was escalating fiercely between the two. It was becoming increasingly challenging to determine who would emerge victorious and who would be defeated. Anishiv was growing weary, so he exerted himself and forcefully pushed Saddhant away. He grabbed a bow in his hand, strung an arrow onto it, and released it towards him. Saddhant mirrored this action. Anishiv's blow failed to hit the target. Consequently, he quickly grabbed another arrow, ignited its tip with fire, and started to spray the volley of burning arrows at Saddhant. Those burning arrows created smoke as well. Consequently, Saddhant was unable to see the number of fiery burning arrows heading his way. He was seriously injured by those burning arrows. Then came Anishiv's lethal strike. He grasped a sword in his hand and lunged at him. At that moment, the memories of his father King Ashan's demise, began to flash before his eyes. The glimpse of Tushyan murdering King Ashan and Queen Kauriya, weighed his heart. Anishiv replicated that act; he too plunged his sword into Saddhant's stomach, leading to his death.

On the other side, King Rahu's general and King Suhadh were locked in battle with each other. The general drew an arrow and aimed it at King Suhadh's chariot. That blow shattered one wheel of his chariot. The commander(general) then dismounted from his chariot and climbed onto his horse. The horse let out a neigh. The general led his horse to trample King Suhadh's chariot. Obeying, the horse charged and crushed the chariot, prompting King Suhadh to leap out of the chariot to save himself. The commander noticed that King Suhadh was unharmed, so he directed his horse once more to trample King Suhadh. In response, King Suhadh swiftly hurled a spear at the general, causing him to crash hard to the ground. After striking the general, King Suhadh sidestepped to avoid the horse's kick. Afterwards, King Suhadh grabbed a bow from his scattered chariot and shot an arrow at the commander, which pierced his chest, resulting in his death.

Following that, Jayan and Parthan came face to face. They engaged in a fierce battle. Parthan shot a fierce weapon at Jayan. Jayan foiled his blow by hurling his spear at him. Then, Jayan invoked his magical abilities and launched another spear at Parthan, which transformed into multiple spears. Parthan also conjured a water shield above his head; those spears struck the shield and shattered. Jayan roared in defiance and unleashed another magical weapon towards him, which similarly multiplied into numerous weapons. It appeared as though meteors were showering down from the sky. Parthan quickly erected another water shield for his defense. However, this new weapon was far more potent than the last, ripping through Parthan's water shield and was about to kill him. At that moment, Sarath noticed Jayan's attack and, in a bid to protect Parthan, swiftly unleashed a massive fireball. That massive fireball engulfed all of Jayan's weapons. Parthan looked at Sarath and beamed with gratitude. Jayan was enraged as his weapons against Parthan were failing. He slammed his fist in frustration. Subsequently, Parthan sprayed a volley of arrows at his charioteer and then targeted his chariot. Jayan found himself powerless and collapsed onto the ground. Parthan, undeterred, continued to rain arrows down upon Jayan, he was determined to prevent him from regaining his composure and preparing to strike back. Jayan instantly grabbed his shield and tried to guard himself from his lethal arrows. Several arrows penetrated his arms and legs, leaving him gravely wounded. He concealed himself behind the shield. Suddenly he felt the onslaught had ceased; when he cautiously lowered his shield, he saw Parthan standing serenely just a few steps away. Jayan was bewildered, but as soon as he spotted the sword lying nearby, he smiled at Parthan and bent down to pick up the sword. With a fierce roar, he charged towards Parthan to deliver the final blow, completely unaware of when he had discarded his shield. Then, Parthan drew an arrow from his quiver, nocked it to the bow, and launched his final blow, striking Jayan squarely in the chest. He collapsed and succumbed to his injuries.

Kishit was slaying Grandsire's soldiers. Aravir witnessed Kishit obliterating a herd of troops with a single strike. Therefore, Aravir made Kishit as his next target. He maneuvered his chariot towards him and began circling around his chariot. Aravir then cleverly bewildered him and shattered his chariot. Kishit found himself powerless. He attempted to shield himself from Aravir's attack. However, one of Aravir's strikes caused him to tumble down from his shattered chariot. After that, Aravir also jumped out from his chariot and handed him a sword.

"We do not exploit others' vulnerable state. Our ancestors never taught us to deceive someone. We are not cowards like your father who used to betray people and attack from behind. We believe in providing equal opportunities to everyone and this is the strength of our lineage! Now come and fight with me!" Aravir yelled.

Kishit growled with rage and assailed Aravir. Aravir also countered his blow and pounced on him. They both were insanely fighting with each other. At one point, Kishit nearly defeated Aravir, bringing him to the brink of death, yet somehow, Aravir managed to defend himself and rose once more to confront Kishit. Neither was willing to yield. The sound of their swords clashing seemed to pierce the ears of the soldiers engaged in the surrounding battle. This brutal conflict left them with numerous deep wounds across their bodies. Ultimately, Kishit's sword slipped from his grasp due to Aravir's overpowering blow. After that Aravir took a bow in his hand, strung an arrow on it and sprayed it at him. That one blow of an arrow stuck in Kishit's stomach. Which made him fall weak, yet his bravery and strength remained intact. He still tried to attack Aravir, and his last blow inflict a wound on Aravir's hand. Kishit wanted to finish him, but he could no longer resist and took his last breath.

On the other side, King Rahu was relentlessly attempting to overpower Grandsire using various weapons and his extraordinary abilities, as he was adept at wielding many arms. However, he understood that vanquishing Grandsire was no simple task. Therefore, he resorted to his enchanted weapons in an effort to eliminate him. Yet, Grandsire was dismantling each of his armaments. King Rahu's forces were dwindling, and his position was growing weaker. All of his formidable warriors had perished. This realization struck King Rahu, making him understand that defeating Grandsire was beyond his reach. Thus, he proclaimed,

"If I cannot possess Glass Palace, then I will not allow anyone else to have it either. Especially you, Grandsire Vasud!"

With this declaration, he signaled his remaining soldiers to encircle Grandsire, then swiftly made his way towards the Glass Palace to obliterate the throne. Grandsire was about to stop him, but his soldiers had already surrounded him from every direction.

'It will take me some time to eliminate these soldiers, and if King Rahu reaches the Glass Palace in that period, it will spell disaster. If the Glass Palace gets destroyed, we will inevitably lose this war; our hard work and long wait of so many years will all be in vain. Our heritage and the last sign of King Ashan and King Harishan will also be lost. I can't afford to let this happen. This whole war happened because of the Glass Palace, now I cannot afford to lose this battle at any cost.' Grandsire thought.

Then he turned to Anishiv and Parthan. "Anishiv! Parthan! Rahu is heading towards the Glass Palace. Go and stop him." He yelled.

During the battle with the other soldiers, Anishiv and Parthan nodded and promptly unleashed their superpowers, swiftly eliminating numbers of soldiers at once. Aravir and Sarath also heard Grandsire's yelling. Therefore, all of them headed towards the Glass Palace while killing every enemy soldier that obstructed their way.

As King Rahu arrived at the Glass Palace, he slammed the palace door open with a loud bang. This noise caught the attention of Sriha, Ashmi, Kasita, Srishtika, and Aparvi, who were gathered in the royal court room. Upon hearing the noise, they spun around towards the entrance and noticed King Rahu was entering into the palace with intense fury. His gaze was set on the throne. As soon as Srishtika and Aparvi noticed this, they quickly came and positioned themselves between the throne and King Rahu.

The atmosphere was thick with tension as King Rahu stood before the fearless ladies, his wrath palpable.

"Get away from my way, else I will not think even once before killing you all," he thundered, his voice echoing ominously through the hall.

Srishtika, her spirit unyielding, shook her head defiantly. "I know what you are willing to do, but I won't let you fulfil your wish." Her resolve ignited a spark in the hearts of those around her.

Aparvi and Srishtika's eyes were blazing with determination. The two young women, steadfast and strong, became a beacon of hope in this dire moment. Inspired by their bravery, Sriha, Ashmi, and Kasita joined their ranks, forming an unwavering line of defiance against King Rahu.

"Glad that you know already! Today I will not only destroy the throne but also the whole Glass Palace. So, just get out of my way!" His anger simmered, and a threatening glint shone in his eyes.

But the ladies stood firm, unflinching in their stance. They refused to move even a bit.

"Alright then, get ready for my deadliest blow!" King Rahu sneered, summoning the full force of his superpowers. The air crackled with energy, a dark storm brewing at his command.

Srishtika sensed the impending attack. With a quick glance around, she nodded at her comrades, they also understood her signal and nodded too. They were not merely defenders; they were warriors imbued with the strength of unity.

As King Rahu unleashed his wrath, a surge of power erupted from the ladies. Their combined forces clashed spectacularly against his attack, creating a blinding explosion of light and energy. The Glass Palace trembled as their powers intertwined. The sheer force of their retaliation sent King Rahu staggering backwards.

In the heart of the Glass Palace, King Rahu's eyes widened in shock as he confronted the formidable powers embodied by the women before him—Sriha, Ashmi, Srishtika, Aparvi, and the fierce Kasita. He was a little frightened but his relentless greed for the palace and the bitter thirst for revenge was still simmering deep within him. Driven by these dark motives, he moved menacingly toward the throne, a sharp sword gripped tightly in his hand.

As he moved forward, Kasita stepped forward with her own sword. Without a moment of hesitation, King Rahu lunged at her. Kasita was also strong, their swords clashed violently. Each strike from Rahu was met with equal ferocity, but he eventually managed to overpower her, forcing Kasita to the ground. He was about to stab her, but all of a sudden, Srishtika intervened and gripped his sword with unwavering courage. Blood dripped from her hand, yet her demeanor remained stoic.

Aparvi, Sriha, and Ashmi rushed to support Srishtika. However, Rahu's brute force proved overwhelming; he swiftly cast them aside like leaves in a storm. He was prepared to strike again at Kasita, but Aparvi immediately shattered King Rahu's weapon into fragments as she possessed the ability to break anything.

Fury ignited within King Rahu. Enraged, he used his superpowers on them, which caused them to tumble down on the ground. With a malevolent grin, he took a central position within the palace and threw his weapon into the air. Because of his superpowers, his weapon split into nine parts, and each part was imbued with destructive power. Those parts were about to fall in the different places of the Glass Palace. Just then, Grandsire, Sarath, Aravir, Anishiv, and Parthan arrived in the Glass Palace. Their eyes fell on the imminent disaster. Realizing the gravity of the situation, they quickly formed a strategic perimeter around Rahu. Grandsire also signaled Srishtika and the other women to fall in a circle around King Rahu."Destroy his weapons!" Grandsire yelled, his voice echoing through the Glass Palace's shimmering halls.

The nine warriors, standing in a circle around King Rahu, resolutely nodded and unleashed their enchanted weapons created by their powers toward King Rahu's nine formidable weapons. With a brilliant flash, King Rahu's weapons destroyed in midair.

They saved their Glass Palace from getting destroyed. The sight left King Rahu in utter shock, his plans crumbling before his eyes. Grandsire, filled with righteous fury, charged at him and pushed him hard to the ground. Rahu groaned in pain.

"You will also get nothing after destroying the Glass Palace?" Grandsire seethed.

Hearing Grandsire's statement, with a defiant grimace, King Rahu managed to stand, his pride barely intact. "If I can't become the king of the Glass Palace, why would I let your descendants take the throne? You're powerful only because of the throne of the Glass Palace, right? So why not destroy its main source of power?"

"What do you mean by 'main source of power'?" Anishiv asked, eyes narrowed in confusion and suspicion.

King Rahu, eyes ablaze with malevolent intentions, proclaimed, "Whoever becomes the king of the Glass Palace, the throne also bestows power. It becomes difficult to defeat the king of the Glass Palace. Grandsire, you will not allow anyone else on this throne but your own bloodline, so if I destroy it, then no one will be the king of the Glass Palace. With that, I will annihilate your lineage too. Afterwards, the world will bow to me as the mightiest ruler!"

Grandsire, unshaken, let out a hearty laugh, his voice echoing through the crystalline halls. "You misunderstand, Rahu. My strength has never hinged on that throne. It was my son, King Harishan, and his friend, King Ashan, who built this palace, a testament to their friendship, not to show people, but they wanted their lineage to remember this and learn from it. This is a legacy for our lineage. The throne may shine, but its power is derived from the king's heart, not the other way around."

He stepped closer, eyes glinting with wisdom. "Destroy the throne if you must but know this: our power does not stem from mere symbols. We wield strength forged through the ages, earned via rigorous penance and sacrifice by our ancestors. And we, the descendants, keep their legacy alive. You think us vulnerable, but it is you who are mistaken. Our true power lies within. We can throw you away without even the throne."

"But you all have definitely got these powers for free. You all have not done any hard penance, right?"

"Ah, that is a pertinent question, King Rahu," Grandsire replied, a slight smile gracing his lips.

"We have indeed received these powers for free, but we can avail the benefits of these powers only when we become worthy of them."

King Rahu smirked and asked, "Do they really know the value of their power and position? They got to know about the Glass Palace only a few years ago. How did they get power so quickly?"

Grandsire chuckled and answered, "You see, while they may have stumbled upon the powers recently, their virtues—integrity, curiosity, and a willingness to learn—have paved their path. Power, as we often forget, is not merely about wielding might; it's about recognizing responsibility."

King Rahu nodded, intrigued. "So, you believe they are worthy?"

"Worthy is a complex word," Grandsire continued. "They have shown glimpses of worthiness through their actions. They revel in learning, not just for themselves but to uplift those around them. Their ability to adapt and absorb knowledge quickly, though seemingly innate."

Grandsire paused for a while and continued, "King Rahu, if you still think that we have received these powers and position without going through any rigorous struggle, then let me clear your doubt, the Glass Palace is not just a symbol; it is a guardian of integrity. True power is not given lightly; it demands respect and understanding. Those who fail to grasp that will find themselves falling short, this throne throws them down, no matter their lineage."

King Rahu had realized that true kingship could never be destroyed by mere ambition; it remained ingrained in the spirit of those who truly understood the essence of power. But the evil King Rahu was not accepting it. He stood glaring at Grandsire, the weight of his inner turmoil manifesting as fury. Anger surged through him; it was a fire igniting the greedy desires that churned within his heart. In a fit of rage, he advanced towards Grandsire with every intention to attack. The elder, however, was quick and wise. He deftly countered Rahu's assault, pouncing back with an energy that belied his years.

The battle seemed to shift, with Grandsire, who was ready to deliver a final blow that would end it all. But in that fleeting moment, clarity struck King Rahu, he recognized the futility of his ambition. So, he immediately joined his palms and said,

"Forgive me, Grandsire! You were right, I should surrender myself. I am accepting defeat." He requested so conveniently that everyone around him appeared convinced.

Grandsire remained watchful, his instincts raising doubts about Rahu's sincerity. But his grandchildren believed in him and tried to convince Grandsire.

"If he is repenting for his actions and asking for forgiveness, then we should give him another chance." Aparvi requested.

Grandsire was not sure about his integrity but still thought to give him another chance. When they all turned to leave, King Rahu, with a malicious smirk, seized a sword lying at his side. In a swift motion, King Rahu lunged toward Aravir, as he was walking behind. Just as the sword neared its target, Grandsire instinctively reacted and gripped the sword's hilt.

"I knew it! You will never change. Now your end has come!" Grandsire yelled, his voice echoing through the royal court.

Afterwards, everyone looked at each other and slightly nodded. They stepped forward, their superpowers igniting around them like a celestial aura. Radiating energy, they formed a powerful line, their arms were outstretched. That view was marvelous!

In unison, they lifted their hands skyward, their powers intertwining above King Rahu's head, creating a dazzling display of magic. The combined force surged downward, crashing into him like a tempest, with a resounding thud. King Rahu collapsed and took his last breath.

After that, they all breathed with relief. Finally, they had won the battle of the Glass Palace. The air crackled with a mix of triumph and hope as Grandsire crowned his grandchildren, their faces glowing with the promise of a new beginning. Parthan ascended the throne as the King of Madhuraj, while Aparvi stood proudly beside him as the Queen. On the other hand, Anishiv took his place as the King of Kushalraj, with Srishtika gracing the throne as his queen.

The Glass Palace, a symbol of their unity, remained their combined property—a sacred space to nurture their dreams. To safeguard this newfound peace, Grandsire made a momentous announcement: Aravir, the eldest among the siblings, was proclaimed the crowned prince of the Glass Palace. Sarath, wise and capable, was appointed as the minister, ensuring the realm would be guided with prudence.

Sriha and Ashmi had become the princesses of Kushalraj and Madhuraj, respectively. Kasita, ever diligent, stepped gracefully into her role as stewardess once more, now serving Queen Srishtika with the same dedication she had shown to Queen Vedarsha. Together, they forged a legacy of strength, unity, and love, ready to face whatever challenges lay ahead.

More Books By This Author

1. Magic is inside the Crystal

The story is about a magical object called Crystal pot which fulfils everyone's wishes. After the death of a Queen she handed over the Crystal Pot to her daughter, but it got stolen by a person. After stealing the Crystal Pot, that person killed the Queen's daughter. But after so many years that girl came again in a modern era. Did she remember anything? Would she take revenge? Or She would forgive him. Read this amazing short story to know what happened next. By the way, the ending will shock you.

The story is full of mysteries and secrets. Readers will find all the flavours in just one story.

2. The Elysia's Rainfall of Tears

This is a short story. A beautiful princess was living her happy life. But an old woman cursed her. The cursed princess caused a flood and her whole Kingdom was destroyed. Then she ran away from her own Kingdom. In her difficult times she found someone to help her and her entire life changed.

How a small innocent girl became a bold woman when difficulties hit her, how the curse turned into blessings and how Oswald's puzzles have added some extra flavours in the story and helped to solve the whole mystery.

It's a very fascinating story. Readers will have fun when they will read Oswald's conundrum.

3. Within you

When people stop listening to their heart, they get surrounded by darkness, sorrows, despair and frustration. They feel lost and disappointed in life. It is very important to hear your own voice. We all possess the answer to our every question and the solution to our every problem, but the thing is that we have forgotten to listen to it. At that point, we might think that we need someone who can help us hear our own voice or that a miracle should happen. Something similar happened with the girl in this story.

There was a girl named Sia who was very ambitious. She wanted to accomplish all her dreams but due to lack of support she couldn't. However, her hope was still alive. She tried to achieve what she wanted, but nothing happened. At last she gave up and decided to go with the flow. She started thinking that everything is over, only darkness has remained in her life. She started feeling that all the doors are now closed for her, but she had forgotten that there is always one door that remains open for everyone. Because when you least expect, something unexpected happens.

A divine light came in the form of a girl to rescue her. The girl made her understand what the actual life is and how to live it. She showed her the power of manifestation and a way to her dreams. Sia used to talk to that girl. But when she came to know about that divine light, about that divine girl, she was astonished. That divine light was residing in herself. After knowing this truth she felt as if she had conquered the world.

www.ingramcontent.com/pod-product-compliance
Lightning Source LLC
Chambersburg PA
CBHW040800120726
48005CB00012B/1250